NO SONG, BUT SILENCE

NO
SONG,
BUT
SILENCE

Hélène Le Beau

TRANSLATED BY
SHEILA FISCHMAN

Coach House Press
Toronto

ACKNOWLEDGEMENTS
Quotations from *Antigone* are from the translation by
Dudley Fitts and Robert Fitzgerald. Translation of the
"Queen of the Congo" poem is by Philip Stratford.

I am grateful to Carole Corbeil for urging me to
read *La Chute du corps.*—Sheila Fischman

FIRST EDITION
1 3 5 7 9 8 6 4 2
Published in Canada 1995
Published in the United States 1995
Printed in Canada

Published with the assistance of the Canada Council, the
Department of Communications, the Ontario Arts Council
and the Ontario Publishing Centre.

Canadian Cataloguing in Publication Data
Le Beau, Hélène
[Chute du corps. English]
No song, but silence
ISBN 0-88910-467-0
I. Title. II. Title: Chute du corps. English.

PS8573.E16C5813 1995   C843´.54   C95–930767–2
PQ3919.2.L32C5813 1995

For Nicolas
With thanks to Smadar and Vanessa

My life spreads out like this; it becomes very fine and transparent as a screen. You can see through me.
~Yehuda Amichai

I was born in Suresnes, a suburb of Paris, in a military hospital devoted to victims of severe burns. Another idea of my mother's, who saw this as her contribution to the war effort. A good ten years had passed since the last war, but they were still finding maimed individuals to patch up, and the hospital needed warm young flesh for its expiatory surgical rites. By way of thanks for the fine care the hospital staff had provided, my mother left her screams and my placenta for the institution's use. A blood-streaked little bundle was deposited in her arms, and then she was left to wait in a corridor. It was a rainy autumn morning, which led my father to give me an umbrella, to earn my forgiveness for his not having been there. It was morning because, in our family, children are always born in the morning at twenty minutes past ten.

I hurt my mother. In the narrow tunnel that would transport me to the attending physician's gloved hands, I already had a hunch that we'd have things to say to each other, my mother and I. I knew I was going to be robbed of some flesh, the smell of swindle marked my passage. I did not want to plaster my placenta onto some burnt body. My father was against it too. He did not understand why we should cross Paris and berth in some unfamiliar suburb, to undergo this process, which he didn't much care about anyway. Women's business, he conceded finally. Did he already know that I was not the one he'd been expecting?

My mother wanted war, and I let her have it, from the moment we arrived at the hospital and parked in the lot for parturients' cars. Since we were alone, no one could later give evidence about the fierce battle that was about to be waged. Moreover, the only one who could be reproached for taking her time was about to lose all her defences. My poor mother was deposited in an improvised labour room where she was visited every hour by a sleepy midwife who refused to get down to work. Is it coming? No, Madame. I'm in pain! Yes, Madame. Do something! There's nothing to be done, Madame. Exhaustion was already overcoming her. She resented me.

8

So did I, and that didn't help.

It took time. The harder she pushed, the tighter I clung. They wanted my placenta? Very well, I'd give them a placenta: torn to shreds and so messed up it would be useless. On my way out I turned myself around sideways. There was resistance for a few minutes, then everything heated up, and I let myself be carried along in the laceration. In any case, my mother had had enough.

She didn't look at me, but I could see what the doctor was doing as he sewed her up. A stitch here, a stitch here, knit one, purl one. A total disaster. He couldn't have cared less about the laceration. He was only interested in the pink bundle he'd collected so carefully for his colleague who worked with the veterans. Fresh meat for the cannon fodder.

I was a girl, not a boy. A little tube going up inside and no descendant to carry the torch. Another disaster. In revenge, they put on a long face and gave me the expected one's name. Stéphane, you see, already had a future, a history, and here I was stealing them from him through some chromosomal dirty trick. After a week in the corridor my mother returned to the fold, empty-handed and ashamed, with a muffled little bundle under her arm.

I spent most of my time on the billiard table that served as both my bed and changing table, except at nursing time and during our walks in the cemetery. Good weather or bad, my mother would take me out for a breath of fresh air among the dead. There was nothing innocent about it. One day she took me to the priest. Rain was falling over Paris. I had my umbrella, she had the look of an ogre. My father was waiting for us at the church, along with a makeshift godfather and godmother. Today is the day to give you a name, they told me, the name of the other one. It was cold, and the icy water in the baptismal font didn't appeal to me at all. Was it really worth catching your death of cold in there just for a name? The whole business took a few minutes. I baptize you in the name of the Father and the rest of the song and dance. And then I peed, right in the middle of my cultural bath. We went home in the rain with a dusty candle and some stamped papers wedged beneath my bottom. My makeshift godparents were invited in for the ritual sugared almonds. I've never seen them again. I don't even know their names.

The three of us had to get organized, I'd been warned: Papa has a thesis to write, and Mama helps him. I used to wake up very early. Very early, too, I learned not to ask for anything, to wait till someone came, hoping they hadn't forgotten me. I would wait for the blue sheets behind the door to stir. I would wait for my father to clear his throat. For footsteps to glide along the hardwood floor, for murmured words, timid laughter. I would wait for the silence that sometimes returned. For the proffered breast that I could knead and for my mother's nervous hand that could never find the right place on my body. I waited, in a word, for time to pass.

I acquired the patience to do so after an episode that demonstrated my parents' indifference more than it displayed my resentment. I was happy, I'd forgotten all about the business with the placenta. One afternoon I was asleep under a mound of blankets when the bell of the church next door began to peal. It was the first time I'd heard such a thing. A monstrous, gargantuan chiming paid for by some religious fanatic in need of a little devotion. The noise shattered my eardrums, it was a call from the devil, my body begged for mercy, I was in pain, I howled. The bell exhausted its song at the very moment when I burst into my own. It went on and on. I knew that behind the closed door of their bedroom they were waiting for it to end. Hours later I had no more breath, no more tears, no voice, no lungs, no desire for anything. As the two of them bent over the billiard table, my father said, It's all right, she won't do it again. All that remained of my cry was a painful hiccup that transformed itself into a cheerful, stubborn laugh, a laugh from the dawn of time when it had been determined that I would be refused forever the right to lay claim to my childhood.

One day they bought a car. The deed had been in the works since my birth. A baby carriage without a car was inconceivable. However, they had to present my father's grandmother, who used to slip us some cash, with a fait accompli. My mother went out to send granny a telegram, and to celebrate we drove off to Chantilly in the second-hand Volkswagen that smelled of dog. When we came home, the concierge handed us a telegram from America that had arrived in our absence. Inheritance not scrap metal stop Return at once stop Funds cut off. From her cheap and nasty New World, the old lady was paying for their education, so my parents had no choice. They managed to negotiate a return after the thesis had been defended. In silence, my mother rejoiced.

We crammed ourselves with Italy on the quiet before the defence of the thesis. A month with no billiards or cemetery. I was forbidden to nurse, on the advice of the doctor who believed that issuing edicts would justify his fees. My mother regretted it because now she was consigned to long sessions of sterilizing bottles. When you're camping there's nothing more difficult. Another of her bright ideas, camping, the other being to have me sleep in the trunk of the Volkswagen, on top of the spare tire, since the tent they'd borrowed from the concierge was just big enough for two, without the suitcases or the camp stove. A postcard.

Every day my mother spread out the equipment for my bottles and stuck to a tight schedule to keep me supplied with milk. Because I refused to co-operate. At the age of one year I still was not eating. There was no way to make me swallow anything but milk, and not just any milk. I'll spare you the fortunes that went into trials of different varieties, more or less skimmed, homogenized, pasteurized, whipped, flavoured with chocolate or vanilla, sweetened or condensed. Eventually I opted for a little added salt. Lukewarm salted milk in a still-warm sterilized bottle: I asked for nothing more.

We were in Florence where I forgot all about my whims and fancies when I discovered the "Birth of Venus" at the Uffizi. I fell in love with it. The sensuality, the slender body, the shell that should have been my own cradle, even the lady's feet: I longed for it all. It was too trite for my father, for my mother too lascivious. I alone, panting with desire, pleaded with Venus to take me along, promising her smooth sailing. My passion would dispel her melancholy. How lovely that lady was! I continued to crane my neck long after they considered the visit to have lasted long enough, craned it until it was ready to break, in the hope of seeing her fingers shudder, leave the modest breast and sketch the sign I was waiting for. I'd have forsaken everything for one second of her love. Her birth would have been my own. No more being the wrong sex. No more cemetery or priest. I would have coiled myself inside her shell and grown up at the side of my beloved. Nothing of the sort happened, and at two o'clock there we were beside the Arno, prostrate from the heat, not knowing where to go in search of shade.

They put me under the olive tree by the tent, decreed a nap; I fell asleep. And then at that very moment they made Malou for me. I sensed right away that something serious was happening. While I slept there had been a great flash, a tremendous illumination, then everything had grown calm. My shell was growing. I was no longer alone! Behind the tent's grey canvas, millions of cells were calling on me for assistance, were setting out on their swift, their unchecked race, because Malou was moving fast, she was flinging herself into life at two hundred miles an hour. My Malou was taking shape, she was settling into her nest. I knew already that, for her, birth would be simple. Life would at least spare her that initial suffering.

My mother didn't realize right away that someone was living inside her. I took advantage of that ignorance to give Malou her first lessons, those that would let her make her way through life. The apprenticeship began immediately after my parents' fruitful nap. The light was slowly extinguished over the distant city. We had slept for a long time. Look, Malou, I told her, look carefully at the sky under the olive tree, see its colour, smell its perfume, because you *can* smell the sky, Malou, it can smell as powerful as you want it to. It smells of its colour: blue, mauve, orange or sometimes green in the evening when melancholy creeps over you. In the morning it's most often grey, but grey, my Malou, grey is the scent of pearls, of milk, of the moon, it drives away all the hungers, all the sorrows of yesterday. Take the sky, Malou, it is yours, it is where you come from, it is where you will return when the earth is turned over upon you. The sky is what you will see most often: the sky of your bedroom ceiling; the sky of the grownups' nostrils; the sky of your carriage;

14

the sky above the Arno, the Seine, the Danube, the St. Lawrence. As many skies as there are days, nights, hours in your life.

Second lesson in life: you too will have a little tube that can't be seen. It will be inside, like mine. I know that. I know that you're a little girl, but it's not so bad because this time our parents have planned it. The second one will be a girl. They said that when I was inside. The first a boy, the second a girl, and it doesn't matter about the rest. With me they were mistaken, while in your case they'll have wanted the little tube inside, regardless of what they say, and you'll hear some good ones. But don't worry, we have a good life all in all, Malou, even better perhaps, because we aren't required to prove ourselves. That is something we do only for ourselves, there's always that, and anyway we couldn't care less about such proofs. And there it is, Malou, my first two lessons in life.

The return trip was difficult. Because of the tourists ogling my mother, my parents were constantly having rows. In our family, rows always take place in silence. Silent tantrums, filthy looks, contemptuous sneers, clenched fists, insults choked back. It's worse than worse. Even when it doesn't concern us we are smeared by it. I had smears of hatred all over my body, along with crumbs of contempt. An endless journey, and Malou got stuck with the battlefield. We arrived back in Paris more dead than alive, and it took a while before I recognized my green baize. It was at that moment that I decided to eat, to speak, to walk. To shield myself from those smears.

I say temetery. It's my first sentence: "I say temetery." What did you say? Temetery. Oh, so that's it! I want to go to the temetery. So you can talk now? Yes, I can talk. You've decided to talk? Yes, I've decided to talk. Isn't it a little early? No, it's not too early to go to the temetery. First of all, what's temetery? It's where I want to go. To the cemetery? Yes. Can't you say Mama? No. Papa? No, I want to go to the temetery with Malou. Malou! Who's Malou? She's my little sister, and I want to go to the temetery with her. Everything else is just babble.

They took me to the Bois and then to the pediatrician. So you don't want to say Mama and Papa. I told him: I'm not talking for you; I'm talking for protection from the smears. He ordered expensive examinations and recommended a disgusting diet, worse than the salted milk. Steak to strengthen the brain and canned spinach because it was the only kind to be found. I'll keep the ferrous taste of it against my palate for the rest of my life. As far as walks are concerned, he added, avoid the cemetery. It's too dangerous.

A few days before our departure for the new country, my father defended his thesis about capitalists and factories. He doesn't defend capitalists in his thesis, my mother would sometimes say, trying to sound interesting. While he was defending himself before the thesis judges, they put me in the cloakroom with the coats. It went smoothly. The defence, I mean. From the looks on their faces when they came to get me, I knew I'd be able to sleep in peace for a few days.

As a farewell present, the concierge's daughter gave me a pair of earrings. We were very fond of each other, Marie Tamponnet and I. It's because of her that my nearest and dearest call me Fanny. The first time I went down to the concierge's lodge, Marie sat me on her lap, bounced me up and down two or three times and then asked me, What's your name? She knew, but she wanted to hear me say it. Stéphane. Stéphane! What kind of name is that for a girl? Stéphanie is one thing, but Stéphane? You really have to be slightly unhinged. I'm going to call you Fanny, and if you like that name I'll give it to you, Fanny-bibi. I dropped the "bibi" but Fanny stayed, except for my parents who never liked it. It was better that way. At least Fanny would not be smeared with insults. When I showed my mother the earrings wrapped in pink tissue paper, she laughed. They're vulgar, she said. Why? Because you'll need holes in your ears to wear them. Holes? Then you'll just have to make me holes. Never! Never will a daughter of mine have holes in her ears. Holes are for whores. Then I'll be a whore.

Silence crept into the room, even louder than my breathing. Everything in the apartment was sold off except my parents' bed and the billiard table. Apparently they belonged to the landlady. For more than a year my father, my mother and I had slept in a bed that didn't belong to us. It gave me a funny feeling when I found out. They held on to the essentials until our departure. The sheets, blankets, curtains, the old Underwood from the thesis and the books had already left in big metal trunks. My father sprained his back helping the movers carry them. Everything else was given to friends. In our family we never sell anything.

All three of us have been sleeping on the bare mattress of the landlady's bed, but tonight I'm alone. Marie couldn't come up; she had a typing lesson so she could become a secretary. Her mother was having dinner at a friend's house. I told my parents not to worry, I could stay on the bed by myself, that I'd sleep in any case while I waited for them to come home. They fixed me brains, *cervelle au beurre noir*, thinking they were doing the right thing—I'd so often turned my nose up at steak—but I couldn't eat it. I hate the smell of meat cooked in butter. I ate the capers on a slice of bread and butter, and they went out. Now silence reigns in the room, and I'm afraid. What if they never come back? Or if they leave on a different boat from the one we're supposed to board at Le Havre the day after tomorrow? Or forget me? Or change their minds? Or decide all of a sudden that with Malou growing, now that they know about her, two girls are too much. It's too much, a girl who talks, walks, eats and turns up her nose when her meat is cooked in butter. What if they don't love me any more? If deep down they've never loved me? Silence reigns in the room, and I don't know if I want to live.

With all the activity in the kitchens, the chef has no time to look after me. He gave me a ball of dough, and I make shapes and one of them looks just like the Little Prince's sheep. I am sitting on a table with my bum in the flour. I like it better here than on the deck where my father is dozing, wrapped in a lap robe. I don't like the deck because I'm not allowed to go near the water. I don't like our cabin either, because of the noise from the motors and the smell of vomit. My mother is seasick. Malou, too, needless to say, even if they claim it's her fault. That's ridiculous. My mother is always seasick, on every sea and every lake and every river on earth. My mother gets seasick in the bathtub, so she doesn't take baths. Only showers, a splash in a flash.

The chef is quite happy to have me with him, as long as I keep quiet. I've been quiet for four days now. Today it's the chef who is agitated because of the captain's birthday dinner. They're planning a big party with an elaborately decorated cake and all the trimmings. A real feast, except that the chef's a nervous wreck. A real celebration to look forward to, except that my mother is vomiting all over the cabin. A real crossing, with waves, except that my father is angry because my mother is such a poor sailor. That's why he's been sulking since this morning on the deck, under his robe, telling himself he's missing a fine opportunity to bring out the dinner jacket he bought in Paris. The only one who's happy is me. My sheep is pretty and I'd like to make one for the captain. Perhaps he'll let me eat at his table. Perhaps he'll let me sample my sheep.

My parents have talked to me a lot about my father's grandmother. They call her the Commander. She has strange little habits, and she has boys. A boy is someone who works in the flower garden or the vegetable garden, who repairs the roof of the big house and the engine of the Rolls. The Commander shouldn't call a boy a boy but she does anyway, it is so chic. She also has a butler, a real one, who wears livery and is the husband of her companion. She is very rich. Her money comes from the workers her husband exploited during the lean years of the Great Depression. Since he exploited a lot of them, he had a lot of money. Now he's dead, he doesn't even know that I exist, and I'm just as glad because we wouldn't have got along very well, he and I. I'm a little afraid to meet the Commander.

They also talked to me about Francine, Papa's sister. Francine has a lot of lovers and big silver rings. My mother thinks she's vulgar. I don't know if it's because of the lovers or the rings. I asked if she had holes in her ears like all vulgar people. My father said I was impertinent. Apparently Francine is very beautiful. She lives in Madrid, San Francisco and Paris. She is in my new city while she's waiting to find a lover. The reason she didn't come to the christening in Paris is because she doesn't believe in God. If I'd known about believing in God I'd never have consented to take my bath in the church. I can't wait to meet Francine. I just know we'll get along very well.

They'll both be there to meet us, the Commander and Francine, when the ship berths. We'll drive across town in the Rolls Royce, and we'll move in temporarily with the boys, the butler and the companion. I must be well behaved and sit up properly at the table, otherwise I'm liable to spoil everything with the Commander. Already she's unhappy because we're bringing back the old Volks that smells of dog and is the reason for our hasty departure from Paris. She has a lot of money, and she prefers Rolls-Royces to Volkswagens; cocktail parties to thesis defences. She has a lot of money, and my mother would like there to be a little for my father when she dies, which should happen soon because she suffers from a serious illness, a shameful disease that her husband passed on to her before he died. But that's something we mustn't talk about, must never talk about in her presence.

My chef is shouting louder and louder. I admire him. With his wooden spoon he carries on like an orchestra conductor. His specialty is pastry in general and gâteau Saint-Honoré in particular. I can't eat any with my parents because of the Paris pediatrician's edicts. My mother has made it a rule, and for years to come, all our meals at home will end with the meat. But in the chef's kitchen, I'm allowed to eat the failed cream puffs, the burnt caramel and, if I've been a good girl, a little sweetened whipped cream. I admire the patience of my chef, despite his yelling. I admire the man who goes from table to table, examining, sampling, sniffing, correcting; the man who waltzes around the food. Everyone likes him. He is fair, and when he says the sauce is too salty, everyone can taste the salt in their mouths.

My best sheep is still waiting on the marble, a little sheep inside a box with silver sugar sprinkles for air holes. I tell my chef I want to give it to the captain, and he smiles again as he did the first time he picked me up in his arms in the dining room. I am the only child on board the ship, and my chef likes children. His own stayed behind on land, far, far away from Le Havre, somewhere in the south of France, and he misses his little girl. He never talks about his wife. Always about little Aglaé and her polka-dot dresses. I tell my chef, When I grow I'm going to be the wife of a chef and a whore with holes in my ears. He bursts out laughing, and we're great friends.

I wish I could stay for the captain's birthday party, but the chef tells me my parents would be unhappy if they had to eat in their cabin without me. He knows about my mother's seasickness. He knows about Malou, too, because I told him. He laughed again when I told him Malou had been made under the olive trees in Florence. You're a funny little girl, Fanny. Because he is allowed to call me Fanny. He and Marie were the first ones I allowed to call me Fanny. On account of my mother's seasickness and Malou, he prepares special dishes. When the sea is smooth and my mother can go to the dining-room, he gives us the table by the window which is sheltered from the noon sun and gives us a view of the sunset in the evening. He knows I like to watch as the ball of fire is extinguished in the water. He knows it has a strange effect on me, as if I could fly away into the ball of fire and be extinguished along with it. Afterwards I'm allowed to visit the kitchens because my parents are sipping their tea. I give everyone a kiss, and I nibble an éclair or a millefeuille.

I will not attend the captain's party. My mother will not touch the plate the chef has prepared for her. My father will take a walk on the deck. He'll smoke the cigar the captain offers him, for his trouble. And I'll go to sleep without having sampled my sheep.

~

The Commander does not come to meet us. Neither does Francine. It always happens, my father says, they must be sleeping. We wait for a taxi with all our gear, then we take two because one's not enough. Since I have a cold I get in the car with my mother who has stopped being seasick now that she's back on land. She is glad to be home. Her new life is waiting for her. Now she can sing in the choir, be a volunteer, play bridge in the afternoon and watch her belly grow. And she's happy because she will have a vegetable garden behind the house my father is going to buy her, furs she'll be able to wear very often, elegant rings—not like Francine's—and who knows, perhaps another child, a real boy this time, whom she'll call Jacques like his father or Henri like the Commander's husband, another child after Malou. I don't envy my mother all those joys to come.

I long to hold Malou in my arms. Through my mother's belly and her suit, it's hard to do. But I can feel her there, all taken up with her task. I can feel her working at life. I can feel that she loves me already, and I love her.

The trees in the city are dry. They won't have any leaves for months. We never go to the temetery. Lightning flashes from the Commander's eyes. Because of Francine. Because of Francine's lovers. Because of me. She says that I talk too much and that it's not normal. She eats meat cooked in butter. I tell her that makes me sick to my stomach, and she grumbles. My father's grandmother says a lot of bad things about a lot of people. Especially her own husband. She says, Good for him if he didn't take his factories to heaven with him. She says she's fed up with workers who want the money that she spends on her Rolls and her cocktail parties. I hate her.

Francine is unhappy. She could talk about it to my mother who is also unhappy, but the two of them don't get along very well. Because of the silver rings. Francine doesn't have holes in her ears, I checked. When I asked why she told me that she couldn't bear to suffer even for one second for two idiotic holes. Even decent people think stupid things. This time Francine wants to go to London where, she says, a boyfriend—and her future—are waiting for her. She'll invite me to her housewarming party. I often sleep in her round bed with her. It stands in the middle of the room. We play swimming-pool. We play I'm drowning, and you save me; we cuddle and cuddle. I'm sorry I can't nibble at her breasts. She smells good. Her cupboards are filled with perfumes and creams and silk stockings. My mother doesn't wear perfume, it makes her head ache. Francine lets me try everything, and I give my opinion about her perfume when she goes out in the evening, to meet another of her boyfriends. It's not really an opinion since I always say Jicky, because I like the name. I dream of looking like Francine when I grow up and of having as many boyfriends as she does, and big rings. Except that I'm going to make holes in my ears so I can wear Marie Tamponnet's earrings.

I've finally met my father's mother. It's hard to believe that she is my grandmother, my father's mother, Francine's mother and the Commander's daughter all at the same time. That's a lot for one person. Luckily she usually lives very far away, in Florida, like all the other people of her kind. I say luckily because life with her wouldn't be a picnic. Life with her would be her, period. With her quirks and her carryings-on as a bonus. The entire planet revolves around my father's mother. As a matter of fact it's due to her that it revolves at all. She has had three husbands, two of whom are dead. With the first, she had my father. With the second, Francine; and with the third, affairs. Of her children she knows nothing because she never took any interest in them. There was Maria, the maid, to do that, and sometimes the Commander, between cocktail parties.

She bounced me on her lap for photos by the Major, her third husband. My grandmother loves to have pictures taken, as long as she's clearly visible. When she smiles she shows all her teeth, which are very straight. She raises her head, which is very blonde despite her age. She shows off her whole bosom, which is very big. I jump up and down and try to see into my grandmother's eyes. She's not interested in mine or in the drawing I made for her. Even though it was a drawing of her, with a big sun like the one in Florence, and an olive tree like the one I looked at the sky through the first time my mother bent over me with Malou in her belly. She didn't recognize herself in the drawing. She told me my cake was very nice. She didn't know a single solitary thing, and I tore up the drawing as soon as her back was turned. She probably won't even notice. Too bad, next time I'll draw a dead fish, and probably she'll think it looks just like her.

For a week now my mother has been spending all day in her bedroom. She avoids my grandmother when she comes to borrow the Commander's Rolls. She avoids the Commander, too. She avoids my father, who has been sleeping in his grandfather's office while he waits for a reconciliation with my mother. Her belly is nice and round, and she cries a lot. It would be better if she didn't cry, because Malou could become accustomed to tears, but she can't do anything about it. My father hasn't bought her the house of her dreams, with a garden. No money. He wants nothing to do with the one that belongs to the workers his grandfather robbed, the one that's used for the Commander's Rolls-Royce and her cocktail parties. I don't think he even wants a house or a garden. He got used to the little apartment in Paris and to driving around in the Volks. He would like that kind of life to continue. Besides, the reason he went so far away for all those years was to escape from his grandfather's bad conscience, for which he has assumed responsibility. That was why he wrote the thesis, to make amends for what his grandfather stole. My mother has just realized that she won't have her house. It's all the same to me, as long as I don't have to eat meat cooked in butter and I don't have to sleep on a billiard table.

~

We have to move. I've ruined everything, as expected. I talked to the Commander about her disease and her companion, whom she treats inconsiderately. I did it on purpose. We've been here for two months, though it was supposed to be just a few days. Francine went away last

Sunday, and my father is sleeping with my mother again. To dry her tears and to stroke her round belly. As far as I'm concerned, I can't take any more of the Commander's high and mighty airs. Her contempt falls on everyone: on her boys, her butler, her companion. Apparently the disease is attacking her brain. I think her brain has always been sick. That was what I said to her. And that she's evil. I told her that, too. That's why my grandmother is the way she is. Super-selfish. She hasn't been to see us since the last photo session. Too busy decorating the new apartment she bought herself in Florida and saying terrible things—as she does habitually—about anyone who doesn't believe that the earth revolves around her. As for the old lady's brain, if you ask me not only is it rotten, it rots everything around it. If we stayed any longer I'd be afraid that Malou might catch that rot.

It's high time for it to stop and for my father to get moving. If he doesn't, I'll find them an apartment. My new grey city has room for millions of people and hundreds of neighbourhoods. We could live in the same neighbourhood as the workers my grandfather robbed. Atone for the wrong he did them by living a normal life. But my mother would be very sad. When she married my father she really believed in her house and her garden. Could she have dreamed about having boys and a butler? I don't know. I don't know her. Anyway, all that matters for me now is to leave here quickly and to go anywhere at all.

Malou is born. I'm happy! So happy! She has almond eyes. Almost like a little Chinese. She's so pretty, I'd like her to stay this way forever. Her nose is constantly moving. She is smelling the world. For the moment, she is smelling the glass walls of her new house. She is very small, and the doctors said that she needed a glass house right away, with plenty of light, so she can grow like a flower. I wonder how they water her and if they use my mother's tears: she has started crying again. Anyway, Malou is the most beautiful flower on earth, and I can't wait till she comes and lives with us, with me, in my new room.

My mother hardly realized it was happening. They'd intended to go to a movie. I asked them to stay; I knew the time had come for Malou to arrive. They thought I was afraid of staying in the new apartment by myself. That was part of it, but I also knew that Malou wouldn't like to be born in a movie theatre, with all the noise and the darkness. I begged them to spend that Friday at home just in case Malou should decide that she wanted to spend it with us.

The day before we had chosen some plants for an indoor garden, inside not outside because as far as my mother's dream house was concerned, that dream was ruined. Where we live there's nothing but brick and asphalt. No trees either. My city is like that. Like a cardboard theatre set. With all kinds of spiral staircases of every colour. Maybe that's why there are no flowers. In the winter, painted staircases last much longer than hollyhocks. The first thing we did was put all the plants in the living-room. I wanted one for our bedroom, but my mother said that plants breathe the air humans need, which is unhealthy. I would have liked to give Malou a violet, to water it till she arrived, then I'd have taught her how to water it, and the violet would have grown along with her. Of course, if plants steal the air we breathe, we certainly won't bring in a violet that might suffocate Malou.

They decided to go to the movie anyway. I wasn't pleased. I kicked the door that opens onto the landing, and it hurt. I don't know how to read yet so all I have to do is talk to the plants. I didn't have to wait very long. My father came racing up the stairs; my mother's water had broken in the Volks; they had to rush to the hospital. I had made them promise to take me and to swear they wouldn't give Malou's placenta to a butcher. Cross your heart. He came to fetch me.

In the car I tell him he's forgotten the bag they had packed for my mother and Malou. My mother says they don't have time because she can feel the head trying to come out through her tube. I'm excited. We all are, but in different ways.

My mother wants my father to stay for as long as it takes Malou to arrive. My father is afraid of blood, afraid of the cries of women giving birth, afraid of fainting and looking like an idiot in front of the doctors who are braver than he is, or so he thinks. My mother clutches his arm. Her fingers go white from squeezing so hard. If she had long fingernails blood would spurt, but she doesn't because long fingernails are vulgar. I took a course with her, childbirth without pain. Huh, huh; huh, huh. My father yells at me to keep quiet. Will you keep quiet!

The seat of the Volks is soaking wet. My mother's dress is soaking wet. It smells funny. We've arrived at the hospital. My mother's not in so much pain after all. She refuses the wheelchair that an orderly offers her. She doesn't want to get it dirty. At the admitting desk, the lady who writes the patients' names in a big register has a funny look on her face when she sees me. Children aren't allowed. Not even the ones who come out through the little tube? They let us in because my mother threatens to have hysterics. This time, the obstetrician is with us. He looks at my mother; he looks at her wet dress; he looks at her belly which is dropping down; and he has my mother put on a stretcher with wheels. And if she gets everything dirty it's just too bad. Labour has started. There's no time to prepare the room; the head is engaged; emergency; they race down the corridor; and you, you stay put.

I stayed put, behind the door. My father came and joined me because he was passing out. I had to look after him. Twenty minutes later, Malou was there. That is, she had left the womb. Except for the doctor, no one has ever held her in their arms. She's too small; she has to grow. If she doesn't grow fast enough, it's possible she'll have to push up the daisies sooner than expected. And that's why my mother is crying. She's afraid of those daisies.

At dawn my father and I go home. The apartment seems very empty. I would rather not sleep by myself. Tomorrow is Saturday, so the neighbour's children don't go to school. From eight in the morning, if the weather is fine, they play cops and robbers on the fire escape that looks into my bedroom. I hate their cries. I wake up thinking there's a monster lurking in my room. My father doesn't want me in bed with him. He doesn't want my nightmares and my fears. He has enough of his own. So I take the violet from the kitchen table, and I sleep with it in Malou's bed.

~

She's here, Malou is here. I'm so happy! She still looks Chinese, and she's always sniffing. Everything in the room is white. The walls, the curtains, the bars on her bed, the sheets, her pajamas, her diapers, her socks, her dreams: all are white. Everything must be clean, spotless, because Malou doesn't like dirt. Malou is afraid of dirt. It's her health, rather, that can't tolerate dirt. Her health is delicate. There wasn't enough warmth in the glass house to make her grow. The doctors decided to let her stay with us, in the house with white walls, in case she might do better there. Good thing it's summer, otherwise we'd have had to put her in the oven to keep her warm.

Summer in my new city is very summery. The sun is back, and it seems to be furious at having had to hibernate for so long. It has come back in force, and it sticks to your skin. It's like the leaves on the trees in the nice neighbourhoods. They've all come back at once. We hadn't even noticed them come out, but already they are yellow from the heat and drought. Now that summer has come it never rains here. It doesn't snow either. I know, it doesn't make any sense to say that it doesn't snow in summer. When it gets too hot we go to the Commander's garden for a breath of air. I sit under the magnolia because of the white flowers it has in the spring. Afterwards, when the petals had fallen, the magnolia grew leaves, but I thought that a flower could get the date wrong and burst open unexpectedly on a branch. The boys work very hard to make the garden pretty. They give me a white rose for Malou. I hide it under the blanket in her carriage. I'll plant it later in the violet's earth.

Malou has a lot of diapers. She needs to be changed very often. Her little tube is very very small. I spread open her slit, and I can see it. It's complicated because the peepee hole isn't where I thought it would be. I thought the peepee hole and the tube that goes into it were the same. It's worse. There's the peepee hole, the little tube, and a small pea. But I'm glad to see something that looks like my own complication.

We have to take precautions when we go to the Commander's garden. My mother has a whole kit in case Malou starts breathing the wrong way, or coughing or spitting. That often happens. Apparently it's normal, and if she stops one day it means that she will grow up. Malou cries whenever she sees the Commander. She hasn't met our grandmother yet. I wonder what she will do when she sees her. Maybe she'll poop in her diaper.

My father has gone away. He left a few days before Malou came out of her glass house. His office is far away now, very far from the house. In the same country, but a different city. He writes to say it's a big office in a big factory, but he doesn't steal money from the workers. In fact he finds money for them. He is the one who talks to the factory bosses when the workers have problems. His grandmother nearly keeled over when he told her about his new job in the union. She said that wasn't why she'd paid for him to defend a thesis in Paris; he could go to hell and take his offspring with him. That didn't stop us from getting a breath of air in her garden, under the magnolia. Three girls can take on one brain that's gone soft.

It's not as hot in my father's city, and in the workers' neighbourhoods, there are lots of trees. The factory spits black smoke, but that's not as dangerous as how much we miss him. As soon as he finds the house of my mother's dreams he'll send for us, and then Malou will be able to get better in the shade of a hazelnut tree. My mother will

34

give her the breast, which Malou doesn't even know yet because of the glass house. I hope that she'll give it to her. It's what I would do in her place. Malou doesn't have to submit to the Paris pediatrician's edicts. There's that at least. She drinks milk that we heat up for her when she wants it. She doesn't often want it, and that's why she's so small, but perhaps if she were given the breast she would improve.

One night she doesn't sleep. Neither does my mother. Malou has started not moving her nose so much, and her almond eyes won't stay open. I know she's not asleep because she makes funny sounds with her mouth, and her hands keep trying to catch something in front of her closed eyes. It's as if she was trying to catch life, and I tell her that life isn't something that can be caught, it's too big. You must go through life on tiptoe. I'll teach her that when she can walk. Meanwhile, I hide under the white sheets, and I observe the doctors who have come to watch Malou trying to catch hold of life. If several of us work together perhaps we'll get there. Perhaps we'll be able to catch a little piece of life for Malou.

~

She has fallen into a hole. She didn't get hurt, we'd taken precautions. It has a strange effect on me, her little body dropping into the belly of the earth. It's not as comfortable as my mother's belly, but she's warm in her draughtproof box. She will be warm all her life. I wish they had got her a glass box like her house in the hospital. They said that glass could break and hurt her. I don't want her to get hurt. She doesn't deserve to suffer in the belly of the earth.

My mother is crying because Malou's hole is too small for her to lie down in it too. My father, who has come home to watch Malou fall, takes my mother's hand. In the other hand he is holding a flower that he throws into the hole. I brought the violet and the dried white rose, and I throw them both into the hole. Two flowers for my flower Malou.

The box stayed at the bottom and the earth that had been off to the side filled the hole. We went to my father's new city, and Malou's little bed stayed behind in the Commander's attic.

~

They talked to me about God. I could remember the cold water in the church and the consecrated candle in my carriage. Because of Malou I don't like God. I can see him everywhere. Terrible words come to me when I think of him. I make up the worst insults. We're both angry. My life has changed since they told me about him. It's darker. Sadder. More serious. Now I'm afraid of having holes put in my ears, and I've hidden Marie Tamponnet's earrings in case it should cross God's mind to take them away from me. After all, he took away Malou.

In my father's city, we finally live in a house with a garden. That ought to calm my mother down. It's too cold to sit in the garden, in the shade of the magnolias. In fact magnolias don't even grow in my father's city. What does grow, apparently, are stunted trees and dandelions, in the summer. As for the hazelnut trees, we'll see next year. December is too soon to talk about them. My parents have taken the books out of the boxes and bought a television set so they can watch Pablo Casals on Sunday morning. That's my favourite programme. It's the only one I'm allowed to watch. Pablo Casals is always angry at his students; when he's happy he gets angry at his cello. If Glenn Gould had programmes on TV he wouldn't lose his temper with his pupils. Glenn Gould has been my hero ever since my parents got a record player. Because of the yellow-and-black cover of the Goldberg Variations album and the hundreds of photos of Glenn Gould. Like him, I sing every note, and my mother tells me that music is sacred, that you must listen to it in silence, religiously. More of her pious nonsense. As if the Goldberg Variations had anything to do with the God who took Malou away from me.

I have to learn how to read. It's the only way to protect myself from God. Or from any holes I could fall into. Reading first, and after that I'll write music. And when I know how to read and when I can write music, then I'll play it. Religiously, if it will make them happy.

Before I learn the notes my father wants to teach me the alphabet. He begins with "a". I ask him to start with the Book because I'm already bored. I want words, phrases, Genesis, Exodus, Ecclesiastes. I'm not interested in the Gospels. God is one thing, but his son is out of the question. So my father begins at the beginning. I close my eyes. I listen. I learn it by heart. I open my eyes; I repeat the words and ask him to correct the order, to exercise my memory. His voice and my voice are like Glenn Gould and his piano. I love my father when he recites the Book. He loves me, I can feel it. I learn quickly. I learn to recognize the pattern of the words and the music of the signs. In the beginning God created the heaven and the earth. And the earth was without form and void; and darkness was upon the face of the deep. And the Spirit of God moved upon the face of the waters. God said, Let there be light: and there was light. And God saw the light, that it was good: and God divided the light from the darkness. And God called the light Day and the darkness he called Night. And the evening and the morning were the first day.

I'm dazzled. *Peter and the Wolf, Little Red Riding Hood, La Chèvre de Monsieur Seguin*: they're all cat pee next to Noah's animals on Mount Ararat. How can you protect yourself from God with Monsieur Seguin's goat, I ask you? When you're two years old you need lots and lots of protection from God.

By Easter I know how to read. I read Exodus to them

around the paschal lamb, and my father is angry because he'd rather I'd chosen one of the Passions. My mother asks him to be patient. Passion will come in good time, she says.

My mother is very nice now. Ever since she couldn't lie down with Malou in her hole, her hands seek mine, and we take long walks along the edge of the ravine behind our house. This winter we saw a great horned owl on the chimney. There had been a heavy snowfall the day before, and we were expecting milder weather. My mother came and woke me early. She wanted to walk on the whiteness, to sink into the fleeciness with me and breathe in the sunlight over the ravine. My father was still asleep when we tiptoed out in our boots. We were like two schoolgirls with our muffled laughter.

Outside, the cold surprised us. I don't know the degrees of coldness so I can only say it was the coldest cold I've ever felt. Cold so dry that the snow, which had been fluffy the day before, cracked like meringue when we stepped on it. The cold was blue, blue like the sky, and the chimneys were exhaling straight white smoke. It was when I was looking at the chimney on our house that I saw him. For a moment I thought he was God, that he was the inventor of day and night, light and darkness, and I was very frightened. But in my Book, God doesn't have feathers. God would never come to the roof of a house to get warm.

I squeezed my mother's hand through her glove. I

must have squeezed very hard, because it startled her. She followed my gaze, and when she saw the king of the northern birds, she got down on her knees in the snow. The great horned owl! she exclaimed. We stayed there for a long time without moving, until my mother couldn't feel her knees. It must be terribly cold in the forest, she said, because the great horned owl never comes where there are humans. And he prefers the night. We're very lucky. No white person in living memory has ever seen the great horned owl. Within living memory, only Indians have had the privilege of meeting him in the forest. Indians don't hunt the great horned owl; he is the guardian of their night, guardian of the spirits of the night. That's what my mother told me as I was squeezing her glove.

The great horned owl trembles on the chimney. A low-pitched hooting punctuates the fluttering of his eyelids over his blind eyes. When my mother straightens up to rub her numb knees, he smells the white mother and her child. Then he unfurls his vast wings, straightens his body imprisoned in the cold, slowly lifts one foot and then the other, and soars through the smoke. He is going back to the forest, perhaps to die. The white man's gaze is fatal.

~

In my city I have two friends. Rajiv Mukerjee and Irina

Kowaleska. Rajiv's little tube is outside, and Irina is like me, she has hers inside. I tell them my name is Fanny. At the Mukerjees' they dry lettuce leaves in the cellar. In the Kowaleskis' cellar—you say Kowaleska for the girls and Kowaleski for the boys and for the whole family—they soak mushrooms in huge wooden barrels. In our cellar we raise mice. Actually I raise them, my mother doesn't like mice. I discovered a mouse hole so I put little pieces of cheese there. My father stopped up the hole one day and I unstopped it. Murderer. One morning there was no cheese left. I put down some more, then I hid all day behind a sack of potatoes. My mother was in bed with a fever, and my father was meeting the boss of the factory about paid holidays for the workers. A mother mouse came out with her babies. I closed up the hole, they were afraid, so was I, and then they hid in the sack of potatoes. The whole family. Since the mice were getting fed they grew bigger, and then the mother mouse had more babies that were both her children and her grandchildren. Now I can pick them up and pet them. Rajiv got bitten by the mother mouse, and he made up a story because the end of his finger was bleeding. The Mukerjees' took him to the hospital because of rabies. I've been bitten, and I'm not rabid. It must have something to do with religion. I'm glad I have a family in a sack of potatoes.

Rajiv is five. He has skin like an Indian's. And he is an Indian, only not a Redskin. I imagine that's because his skin is brown. He will learn Sanskrit when he's older.

In the meantime I'm teaching him to read the Book. Recite after me, Vanity of vanities, saith the Preacher, vanity of vanities; all is vanity. What profit hath a man of all his labour which he taketh under the sun? One generation passeth away, and another generation cometh: but the earth abideth for ever. At first he was jealous of my Book, but I told him I'd never learn Sanskrit unless he taught me. That made him proud, and he forgot about being jealous.

I would like it if Rajiv became a chef later on. I could marry him. Some day I'll tell him about whores and holes in your ears. It won't be hard because his mother has holes in hers. I suppose she's a whore. I showed her Marie Tamponnet's earrings. She thought they were very pretty. Or so Rajiv told me, because I don't understand the language Madame Mukerjee talks. It must be Sanskrit.

Rajiv showed me his tube. I've never seen my father's so I can't compare them. I asked him to make peepee. It's disappointing. Why did my parents make such a fuss about a tube that leaks? Rajiv wanted to see my breasts. Apparently all girls have breasts. I guess I'm not a real girl, because I don't. We compare the brown spots on our chests. My skin is whiter, but my spots are darker. Where do you come from, he asks me. From a military hospital. He's not impressed, but he says that explains everything. I have no idea what he is talking about, and I don't care. Rajiv is my confidant. He knows about the mice. He knows about Malou. He knows about Francine's lovers, and he knows that I want to marry him later on. I decided to tell him about the placenta they stole from me when I was born. I've never told anyone about it except Malou, through my mother's belly. I talked about it to the violet that is on Malou's box in the big hole that's too small for my mother.

At first Rajiv doesn't believe me. He says it's impossible that they took my placenta and plastered it onto someone's damaged skin. But it is true, it's as true as the sun. Someone in this world is walking around with a piece of my flesh on his body, maybe even on his face so you can't recognize him, and I'd very much like to meet him so I could tell him what I think. I'd put his eye out. Rajiv thinks it's better to use a placenta than to throw it in the garbage or keep it in the fridge, just in case. That makes sense, but I wish they'd planted it in a garden where it would feed the flowers. Placenta flowers must be as pretty as the mandrakes that grow at the foot of a gallows. I still want to see what he looks like, the person whose skin I'm stuck to. Rajiv promises that our children's placentas will go to fertilize the trilliums we found in the ravine behind my house.

Irina is also five years old. Together the three of us are twelve, nearly thirteen if you count the months. She's not the little sister I'd have liked, first of all because she's bigger than I am and then because nobody, nobody can ever replace Malou. Still, she's the little sister of her three brothers. Last year, her mother went back to her village

43

in Slovakia with a man. Irina became the woman of the house, with a lot of responsibilities. Monsieur Kowaleski is a worker in the factory where my father works. He's a worker who earns more money now that my father speaks in the name of the workers. He admires my father, and I admire Irina's father. His hair is all white, and his eyes are slanted, like the eyes of his Mongolian ancestors, he says, laughing. He always laughs and sometimes he plays chess with my father. The other day a machine mashed his little finger, and it had to be amputated. He laughed till he cried. That's an expression I heard about people who cry and laugh at the same time. We brought him a bouquet of dandelions that we put in his tooth-brush glass, and Irina promised to look after the vegetable garden during his amputation. I was very happy because Irina slept at our house. We put my mattress on the floor, and I slept on the box-spring. That night, before bedtime, I read her a passage from the Book, from Judges, the one where they talk about hospitality. I told her she could ask me for anything, even to go away with my father, and I would grant it to her because she was a guest in the house.

My mother fixed us noodles the way I like them. When Irina's father came home from the hospital with one finger missing I was glad, but I cried a lot. I, too, can laugh until the tears come. They gave me a bunch of carrots for my trouble. I have to say, I did work hard with Irina in the vegetable garden.

~

You're going to have a child. That was how they announced to me that my mother was pregnant. Because you're a big girl now, he'll be your son a little. They're a fine pair of idiots, the way they carry on about sex. And what if it's a girl? And what if I want nothing to do with that child, that little brother or little sister? What about that?

I know about it because her stomach's getting rounder, because peace prevails, because of Malou's bed that they've gone to get from the Commander's house. It's not because the Commander died that they went to get the bed from her attic. It's because of the child. Girl or boy, I want nothing to do with it. I don't want any more glass houses or violets at the bottom of a hole. I sulk, I abandon my Book, no one but Rajiv and Irina understands me. If I were God's friend I'd be angry at him for allowing such a thing to happen. But I'm not God's friend, I'm the friend of Rajiv and Irina, and to hell with God.

~

Francine was here, back from London without her boyfriend and her future. She saw her mother. Those two only see each other at weddings and funerals. The Commander died all alone. The week before, in a fit of

45

rage she had sent her boys, her butler and her companion packing. They were used to it. They always took advantage of it to air out the house in the country. They'd spend a few days there dusting and hoeing the vegetable garden, then she would summon them back so the butler could drive her to one of her cocktail parties in the Rolls-Royce. She never went to her big house in the country. She hated the country. It reminded her too much of her poor, unhappy childhood when there were no cocktail parties or boys.

It was the butler who called my father one night; I had been in bed for a long time. We are in the country, he said, and we haven't heard from Madame for ten days, that's not like her. They had finished the dusting some time ago, and as for hoeing, they'd decided not to bother. With the snow, it's not very practical. So they waited, twiddling their thumbs, for the old lady to call them. The companion, who is also the butler's wife, started to worry. A week before Christmas, with all the cocktail parties on her schedule: it didn't seem right. They'd started phoning four days ago and for four days now there's been no answer. They called my grandmother in Florida, and she told them to call my father.

It was awkward for him because of the disagreement that went back to his new job with the union in the factory. He hadn't seen the Commander since the time she told him to go to hell, not even when Malou was dropped into the hole, and then it was his turn to tell her to go to hell. If my calculations are right it's been more than a year and a half since my father has considered his grandmother as dead. In actual fact she's been dead for four days, and when my father opens the door of her house a charnel-house smell will clutch at his throat, so strong, the carpets and the wall hangings so imbued with it that in years to come he won't be able to call it to mind without blanching. The shameful disease of the Commander's husband had got the upper hand. A shameful disease that gives off a noxious smell.

They brought in the doctor to certify the death and then the morticians and the disinfectants. After two days we were finally able to sleep in the dead woman's house. They let me have Francine's round bed because she didn't arrive till the next day. I opened all her flasks of perfume. My father and mother spent their time packing boxes. They had to empty out everything, give away everything, sell the house. I would have kept the magnolia tree. In a small box hidden in the bottom drawer of the dresser they found the will. A page of nonsense, full of mistakes. Nothing for my father, nothing for my mother, nothing for me, nothing for Francine, nothing for the boys, the butler, or the companion, nothing, nothing at all, and everything to her darling daughter who in turn will leave nothing to anyone when she dies.

She arrived on the day of the funeral, and she left on the day of the funeral. We spent Christmas without her, in the nearly empty house, with Francine who couldn't afford a return ticket to London, and the boys who had been given their notice and a little money that my father borrowed from the bank. I didn't get any gifts that year. Funerals are expensive. Funerals in an empty church with a choir and bells ringing for half an hour, which undoubtedly isn't what she had envisaged. Her body was burned because it smelled so bad. Anyway, you can't dig a hole in frozen ground. They put the ashes in a box, and the box was deposited beside her husband's ashes in a house for the ashes of the dead. I wonder what they say to one another, ashes to ashes. If the ashes of the workers the Commander's husband had robbed were put with theirs, would there be a great battle of the ashes? I'll ask my father some day.

~

You're going to have a child in May. I hope the child won't fall into a hole. I hope I can teach the child to read the Book very early. At last, after many arguments with Rajiv and Irina, we've come to an agreement. Irina has three big brothers, Rajiv has a little brother and a little sister, it's time for my family to grow. By myself, I won't hold out very long. If they could give me two at once it would be even better.

I ask my mother to make me two, two children. My mother, who doesn't often laugh, bursts out laughing. Two! Yes, two! Two boys or two girls? It makes no difference, two girls or two boys or a girl and a boy, just as long as there are two. One after another, would that suit you? Obviously I'd rather have them together, but if there isn't room in my mother's belly I'll take them one at a time. I try to listen through her navel. I don't hear anything. Whatever is inside isn't as talkative as Malou.

They made the child on the first day of school, I remember. My first day of school. I was wearing a dark-green uniform, but I would have preferred a polka-dot dress in memory of Aglaé, the chef's daughter. On the first day and every day afterwards I put the Book in my schoolbag. I can't get along now without school, my schoolbag, the Book and my parents. The reason I go to school is because my father, in spite of all his efforts, hasn't yet been able to teach me how to write. He's despondent, and my mother tells him that's what school is for: to relieve parents' despondency. There are teachers who specialize in writing, who can teach a child who can already read how to write. We'll soon see if those specialist teachers are any smarter than my father. I go to school willingly. I refuse to let them walk me there. I know the way. Rajiv and Irina and I have walked to school and home a hundred times. Rajiv and Irina go to another school, in another language. I speak the language of the Book, and I want to write in the language of the Book. We'll still see each other on the way home, because we've decided to wait for each other outside the kindergarten.

I don't learn how to write on the first day. I'm very

disappointed. What kind of school is this? They give me a desk by the window. Outside, there is a tree. When I've had enough of Mademoiselle Edith, I shall look at the tree. On the desk someone has carved inside a heart: Hélène loves Pierre. It wasn't me because if we're caught carving on our desks we're expelled. Luckily I can't write yet, because I would have carved: Pierre and Hélène are imbeciles. At the end of the day I pack up my pencils and my Book as if I'd been doing it all my life.

I am the youngest one in my class. I'll always be the youngest one at school. We had to give our names and ages in turn. Mademoiselle Edith checked them off as soon as she had found the pupil's name on her list. Everyone is five or six years old, like Rajiv last year and this year. I'm not proud to say that I'm three and even less that my name is Stéphane. I nearly said Fanny but I caught myself at the last minute. That way the girls who get on my nerves will call me Stéphane and the ones I like, Fanny. We'll see about Mademoiselle Edith, I'll give her a few days. When we leave, the others make remarks about my oversize schoolbag. They're just pretexts to humiliate me. It's always like that when you're the youngest.

I run down the lane that leads to the kindergarten street. Esther, a girl in my class, follows me. She doesn't say anything, but she runs with me. When I stop, she stops. When I turn around, she turns around. When I start to hop up and down to see what she will do, she hops up and down to show me. We don't say a word to each other, not hello or see you tomorrow, but I know that tomorrow Esther will be the first and perhaps the only one who will call me Fanny.

~

Rajiv and Irina are waiting. So, do you know how to write? No. They're disappointed, too. We go home with our heads hanging, in silence.

About my child, I know now that it happened while I was on my way home from school with my head hanging. My father had taken the day off. The first day of school in a new school is something for a father. He's not used to being alone with my mother. They put their time to good use. That's why I say that school is as much for the parents' convenience as for their inconvenience. My mother was as red as a peony when I went into their bedroom. Bah! It's not the first time you've slept together I say, to put them at ease. Yes, but this time it's during the day. They've forgotten that they made Malou during the daytime too, and what's more, inside a tent. I am too absorbed by my desk, my pencils, my schoolbag and all those things that make for unforgettable memories of your first day of school to think about the consequences of this second fruitful nap. I take out the list of supplies required by Mademoiselle Edith and I ask my mother to embroider my name on a napkin for lunch at school. In the refectory they don't give out napkins, only milk, and even then we have to bring a tin cup that we rinse in cold water afterwards.

I've discovered something terrible. The first year in my new school is of no use whatever for learning to write. It is useful for "socializing" children. They're absolutely wacko. I feel like a prisoner, and I talk to Esther about it. Esther is an angel from heaven. She consoles me, and she teaches me how to write. Esther has never read the Book, but she knows how to read and write. She even knows how to do amazing things with numbers, how to transform them. She calls it division and multiplication. It helps me understand what's going on in my mother's belly with the new baby. It helps me understand the multiplication of the loaves and the fishes that my father keeps talking about, even though I tell him I'm not interested in any stories about God's son.

She puts the pencil in my hand and traces letters on the paper with me. Real letters that begin, Dear friend and end, Cordially, Fanny. Since she's the only one who knows how to read in this class where the pupils are busy at something else, it's inevitably to her that I write these letters. Together we write on a sheet of paper: Dear friend, Cordially, Fanny. I fold the paper and give it to her. She has several like it that she reads in bed at night, before she falls asleep. She says that if she hadn't met me she would have suffered a great deal. And so would I. I don't want her to write to me. For the time being all I want to read is the Book. Esther doesn't know the Book.

During recess I take it from my schoolbag and open it to a page, any page, so I can teach her how to protect herself from God. She has reservations. She thinks God is good. I tell her that protecting herself from God doesn't mean that God isn't good, but it prevents God from being divided because of men. In fact, protecting oneself from God means protecting oneself from mankind.

I make a pact with Esther. We won't have any secrets from each other until our dying day. What's more, she will be the godmother of my child, that is, of the child my mother is carrying, and I'll be the godmother of her next child, that is of the child her mother will perhaps carry one day. If they are a boy and a girl, they will marry each other later. If the children are the same sex, then I'll marry one of her brothers, if he becomes a chef. But I'll have to talk to Rajiv about it, because of my promise. I've brought a very sharp knife to school, and I make a cut on my finger. I tell Esther to do the same. That's so we can mingle our blood. She doesn't hesitate. Now Esther is my life's companion. My companion for life.

We conclude our pact shortly after the Commander's death and the announcement of my child's imminent arrival. Esther isn't acquainted with death. Or with life, because she has never seen anyone being born. I tell her about Malou's glass house. I tell her about the smell of the old lady too. She finds it hard to believe that a dead body stinks and that they put little girls in glass houses. I don't talk to her about my little tube. Esther is a prude. I think we're more prudish when we're six than when we're three. I envy her her age. My father always says that wisdom comes with age. Esther is very wise. I'm one head shorter than she is. One head less of wisdom, too. But she loves me all the same, and I love her even more because she's teaching me about life.

In the schoolyard the other day, a girl in our class stuck her tongue against an iron bar on the fence that separates the big children's yard from the little children's. Everyone but Esther got worked up. The girl wanted to lick the iron the way you lick an all-day sucker. It was so cold out, her tongue stuck to it. Esther went inside the school, even though we're not allowed inside during recess, she asked for a glass of warm water, not too warm, then she came out again. Very slowly she poured the water onto the girl's tongue. It came unstuck by itself, like a stamp. A little bit stayed on the iron, with some blood, and then everyone went inside because the bell rang. Now Esther is the school heroine.

I've known Esther since the first day of school in my first school. This is the day my parents chose to make a child for me. I'd like it if, in honour of all that, my mother's daughter could be called Esther, like Esther. If it's a boy I'd like his name to be Esther, too.

~

It's beginning again: Esther is born. She's a girl, and she

54

arrived by herself. My parents didn't want to call her Esther like Esther. The name of Esther my-little-sister-my-child is Anne. It's very pretty, but I prefer Esther.

She is chubby and cheerful. She moves from my mother's belly into her arms. No glass house for Anne. She sleeps in my room. I didn't put violets on her mattress because there aren't any here in my city. In May there are only dandelions on the lawns, and dandelions leave stains. On the day of her arrival I draw a great horned owl for her and pin it to the wall above her little bed which was Malou's before. Above it I write these words: *Who is riding so late through the dark and the wind? It is the father with his child.* As soon as she is ready to walk I shall teach her to dance the dance of the great horned owl as he returns to the forest. She will teach me how to laugh. It's what she does best. I soon realize that I can no longer get along without her laugh. She doesn't erase the memory of Malou. She enriches it. Esther gave her a teddy bear. I didn't have a teddy bear, and I'm very glad for Anne. My parents don't spend my father's salary on teddy bears. I thank Esther warmly. I wish she had given me one when I was born. But I didn't know Esther when I was born. It doesn't matter, I have Marie Tamponnet's earrings.

~

I come first in my class. Esther comes second. In his

school, Rajiv comes last. That's because he thinks in Sanskrit. Irina consoles him, she comes last, too, because of all the housework she has to do as her mother's replacement. She has no time for homework. I have introduced Esther to Rajiv and Irina. We are the three musketeers and d'Artagnan. We take turns being d'Artagnan. When my turn comes it's the beginning of summer holidays. We explore the ravine behind the house where everyone is afraid to go. That's because last year a woman jumped in the river, and they found her body further down, near the dam that makes electricity. She had taken off her shoes and socks. But they only found one shoe on the rock that she'd dived from, and a dirty sock rolled up inside her shoe. I didn't know her. No one knew her, and no one could recognize her because the water made her body swell up. When it's my turn to be d'Artagnan, we'll look for the other shoe with a sock rolled up inside it. I would like to know the name of the woman who threw herself into the river. When you have a name you can imagine a face, a life, the people who knew her and who are responsible for her death. It can't be otherwise, it has to be the fault of people she knew, because no one jumps into the river on account of strangers. I wouldn't, anyway.

Mosquitoes bite our legs and arms. The three musketeers and d'Artagnan look as if they have the pox. We find some mushrooms but no shoe or sock. The winter washed away her footprints by the river. Our search is difficult. Esther gets stung by a hornet as well as by the mosquitoes, and she who never says one word louder than another starts yelping like a fox. I scoop up some mud and slap it onto the sting, which is still sucking. It gives her some relief. I can be cool-headed, too, sometimes. We go home empty-handed. The expedition yielded nothing, and I think, that's a very bad way to begin our summer holidays and to celebrate my success in school.

~

My father has changed tremendously. Now that I know how to write he's stopped reading the Book with me. He doesn't talk to me about God's son any more, and that bothers me. He no longer makes faces over Anne's bed to make her laugh. He doesn't speak to the boss of the factory so often because he doesn't go to work so often either. He doesn't play piano duets with my mother any more. Like Malou, he doesn't eat very much. When we leave the table, his food ends up in the dog's dish, and the dog is getting fatter every day. He only talks to me now to insult me and send me to my room.

One day my mother tells him he's too cruel to me, that he should solve his own problems before it's too late. At this rate I'll be crazy when I grow up. Crazy like he is when I'm grown-up like him. Because he's mean. I heard her say that to him from the top of the stairs where I'd gone to hide during dinner yet again, with my plate of steak and canned spinach on my lap. I wondered if she was really talking about me.

He goes for long walks in the city, in undesirable neighbourhoods, according to my mother. He looks up and talks to the gables of houses. Sometimes he takes a stiff-bristled brush and breaks it on my backside. He's right when he says that I'm insolent and impertinent. I stand up to him. I mock him. I provoke him. I want him to react, to get rid of the anger and sorrow that are locked inside him and make him so unhappy. It's the least I can do.

One day my mother fills a suitcase with beach towels, bathing suits, shovels and rakes. We go away. Without him. In the car I keep an eye on Anne and the dog. The dog was one we found after Anne came. My mother was looking for a present to give me to congratulate me for doing so well in school. She asked me what I wanted. I said a dog. The two of us went to see a farmer who lived nearby. The dog was very skinny till he came to live with us. He eats our scraps because my mother can't stand waste. He eats all my father's meals. The dog's name is Gandhi, in honour of Rajiv. Gandhi is Rajiv's hero, but our Gandhi doesn't like yogurt. That's his only flaw because my mother makes a lot of yogurt. It's good for you, and we eat it three times a day, except when a batch doesn't work out. I hate everything that's good for you.

She is taking us to the water. I hope it's not to the shore of the river that carried away the body of the unknown woman last year. You never know, she might want to throw herself into the river, with the Volks and the children. She reassures me. We're going to see Uncle Aimard and Aunt Emma who aren't really my uncle and aunt, but they're very nice people who have taken pity on us. Uncle Aimard and Aunt Emma are almost as old as my grandmother and the Major.

When my mother tells them she can't take it any more, Uncle Aimard tells her to come over and bring the whole menagerie. He sets us up in a little house on the water behind their farm. They raise mink. I don't understand raising mink. There's a field of them as far as you can see. You can hear them squealing and trying to tear the wire-mesh of their cages. They are happier in winter than in summer because of the fur that keeps them warm and the wind that blows the scents of their homeland down from the North. You can't go near them in summer. The smell in the mink field is unbearable. Aunt Emma insists that we eat all our meals with them, in the other house that looks like a white castle except that it's a castle made of wood. I like them all right, even if we have to eat in silence. Uncle Aimard can't stand noise. It's hard to eat in silence with Anne singing. Often they leave us in the kitchen with Mathilda, the daughter of the farmhand who helps Aunt Emma in the vegetable garden, and we eat in silence with my little sister's cooing. It doesn't disturb Uncle Aimard because we close the door.

My mother is sad. Aunt Emma's raspberry syrup doesn't bring back her smile. She misses my father who talks to the walls and gables in undesirable neighbourhoods. Sometimes when she can't stand it any more she calls him. She asks him if he's washed his shirts or talked to the manager of the factory. He must say harsh things to her because every time, she wipes away a tear as she puts down the receiver.

I give sugar to Marianne and Cybèle. I'm afraid they'll eat my hand along with the sugar. I give them flowers too, and when Aunt Emma's back is turned, I pick strawberries for Marianne, the reddest, juiciest ones, and she polishes them off in no time. Cybèle doesn't like strawberries; she's a difficult mare. Besides, Aunt Emma doesn't want me to ride her. But I can ride Marianne, wedged in between her mane and Aunt Emma's tired bosom. We walk along the paths in the woods, behind the mink field. The horses don't like the mink when they squeal. You have to go along the field at a walk so the animals won't get over-excited. Anne is too small to know the joy of the wind in your hair and Marianne's damp breast when you urge her into a gallop. Gandhi comes with us all on our walks. In spite of his weight, he runs fast. I think he's in love with Marianne. He hasn't been eating so much since we've been here. That's to be expected, there aren't any table scraps at Uncle Aimard's and Aunt Emma's house. Gandhi eats from the same bowl as the dog that stands guard over the herd of goats. It doesn't look very tasty, but his appearance is better.

I learn how to swim. The water is cold, but it doesn't bother me; on the contrary, it reminds me of my religious bath in the church. I'll be four years old in a few weeks, and I know how to swim with my arms coming out of the water and then going back in. I spray water all over. My mother says I'm like a fish in the water, and I feel as if I'm inside my mother's belly. In her belly I wasn't a fish, I was a little girl who should have been a boy.

Anne sleeps on the sand. Sometimes she eats it. We know because there's sand in her diaper. She makes sandy poop. I have trouble with my sand-castles because Gandhi drops his big paws on my turrets. Gandhi likes the water too. He swims better than I do, and longer, and he brings us all the branches floating on the water. Uncle Aimard makes big piles of them that he'll burn in a huge bonfire in the fall.

I wonder if my mother is going to keep her promise to me and make the other child right after the last one. I keep an eye on her stomach. Instead of getting bigger it's shrinking. I don't say anything about it to her, but I'm worried. If she puts it off for too long, I'll have to do it in her place. I tell Esther about it in my letters, but I don't know what she thinks because I've forbidden her to write me. I still refuse to read anything except the Book. Thank goodness for the Book! It protects me from my father's absence. I miss him a little all the same. Quite a lot, and

I can't wait to go home, to see him again, to see Esther and Rajiv and Irina. They'll be waiting for me to play the three musketeers and d'Artagnan, even though it's Rajiv's turn to be d'Artagnan. They promised me before I left, and now that we've mingled our blood, I believe them. We mingled our blood on the day I left, with the same knife I used to mingle my blood with Esther's. Now there are four of us who have mingled our blood. When Anne is big enough we'll be five, if she wants.

We are going home. The holidays aren't over, but we're going home. With Mathilda, who is coming along to help my mother. The hospital phoned. My father doesn't talk any more, that's why the hospital phoned. How can you expect my father to phone if he doesn't talk any more?

~

My mother must have said: It's Stéphane. He didn't recognize me. He hugged Anne very tightly, and she started to cry. That was during his first leave from the hospital. I had gotten used to living with his absence, with his shadow on my mother's face whenever she came back from seeing him.

The doctors authorized his leave. A weekend's grace. I went with my mother to get him. I waited for them in the car. I didn't recognize him either. He looked like someone else: a younger man, smaller, with muscles like a child's. As if he was my father as a little boy, before he grew up. He who never showed any surprise would exclaim at the slightest thing: What a lovely neighbourhood this is, and the trees, like bouquets of broom; your ratatouille smells good, do you remember Florence? He had the eyes of a child, and he didn't recognize me. She's your daughter, my mother added.

Monsieur Kowaleski came to see him. On behalf of all the workers at the factory he offered best wishes for a speedy recovery. And then they played chess, even though Monsieur Kowaleski is missing his little finger. A little finger doesn't matter in chess, as long as you aren't missing a little piece of brains. My father must have had all of his because he won.

Irina talked to me about her mother while her father and mine were playing chess. She certainly took her time, I've known her for nearly two years! I didn't imagine her mother like that at all. Prejudices are funny. It's the same for the woman who jumped in the river. You get something in your mind because it suits you and then one day you discover it has nothing to do with the truth. As far as Irina's mother is concerned, I'd pictured her as ugly, fat and mean, because my own ideal mother is beautiful, slender and nice just now, except on days when I'm angry. Irina's mother is all of that: beautiful and kind and so on and so forth. I'm sure Irina was exaggerating. She saw her for a month this summer, in her native village in another country. Even her second father is handsome, and he has a heart of gold. They gave Irina a bicycle. She brought it back on the plane with her, which was no small matter. Irina met her cousins and her four grandparents. Six, actually, because of her second father. Everyone was nice. She didn't want to come back, but she came anyway, because of the three musketeers and d'Artagnan, she said. I believe her.

It was the first time she had seen her mother since she went back to her native village with another man. An airplane ticket and a bicycle are expensive, and Irina won't go again until she's ten. A four-year wait. Next year it's Jan's turn. That's a long time—three brothers—before you can see your mother. If I could, I would give her a plane ticket every day so she could go back to her mother's native village.

We have to cut his meat and vegetables into little pieces. The doctors warned my mother: Chewing is difficult and his hand is lazy, because of the pills. Spinach is all right, it's soft. I asked my mother not to cut my steak. I can cut my steak all by myself. She gives me a plate covered with pieces of steak already cut up to show me she's the one who makes the decisions. If you don't like it, go to the kitchen and do it yourself. I don't like it. I go to the kitchen. There are some pieces left on a board. I pick up a big red one and swallow it, to take my revenge. Without chewing. It doesn't go down, of course, and the room spins, I can't breathe, that was incredibly stupid. My mother must be worried that I haven't come back.

She'll save me, as mothers always do. She comes. I fall. She doesn't panic. Her hand roots around at the back of my throat, gropes a little, finds the piece of meat and pulls, faster, I can't take any more. At last, triumphant, she brandishes it above my head. She is exultant. As if to say, I told you so. It would have been better if I'd died completely. Back at the table, I see my father take the pieces of meat from his plate one by one. It's disgusting. I vomit, and I'll never eat steak again, not in this house or anywhere else, raw, cooked, cut, chopped, or whole. Steak is degrading.

He was sitting in the garden. I told him about Marianne and Cybèle and our holiday at Uncle Aimard and Aunt Emma's. He listened. It was the first time I'd really talked to him about me, about what I'd done, about what I was thinking during the time he was away. He listened, and he smiled. I even brought him a glass of water and the pills he has to take. He drank without complaining, though he had never taken an aspirin in his life. I watch him. My mother told me he'd had electric shocks to chase away the dark thoughts he had inside. I try to imagine the electricity that activates the dark thoughts, and I wonder where they come out. Through the nostrils? It can't be through the ears because his ears are too small for his enormous dark thoughts. Through the mouth then? Can you make dark thoughts come out through your mouth? That night I position myself under my bedside lamp with my mouth wide open so the dark thoughts can escape. I don't see anything. All that happens is that I feel like saying dirty words. The next day my thoughts are still just as dark and my father has to go back to the hospital.

~

The priest is dead. The one who plunged Anne into the cold water in the church. Esther and I go to see him. He has hair in his ears and flowers around his body. Esther tells me it's not true that corpses smell bad, because the priest's corpse smells like flowers. I tell her that if they took the flowers away he'd smell like the Commander.

We kneel beside the table where they'd put him. His face is waxy like a hardwood floor. He came to see us at school last year with some missionary nuns from Africa. In class I asked them if missionaries can choose their countries in Africa. My classmates laughed. I didn't ask the other question I was dying to ask, because of my classmates' idiotic laughter. I'm sorry now, because I'll never know the answer. A dead priest can't tell me if there are missionary chefs in Africa.

Esther is still my best friend at school. On the subject of the other child my mother is supposed to make me, she tells me to be patient. That children aren't born in two days. Who does she think I am? I know perfectly well that children live in their mothers' bellies for nine months. So what does she mean, be patient? For years?

Now is when I need another child. To chase away my dark thoughts.

"My daughter? My daughter's name is Anne."
"Come on, Papa. Don't you recognize me?"

Gandhi fawned on my father because of the plates of food he never finished. It was pointless, though, because now my father cleans his plates with their little piles of cut-up meat and vegetables. Gandhi has been much better since he stopped eating table scraps. He brought a baby cat back from the country. One day, out of the blue, he was carrying one of the barn kittens in his mouth, and ever since they haven't been out of each other's sight. We don't know yet if it's a boy or a girl, but we've called it Ali. They're inseparable. As soon as my mother turns off the light in my bedroom, Ali and Gandhi jump onto my bed, and we all sleep together.

The first night, the light in their bedroom stayed on very late, and my mother talked for a long time. Actually I think my mother was talking all by herself. My father said nothing; I didn't hear his voice. He is here for two nights, and on Sunday he'll sleep at the hospital, between sheets ironed by the nuns. I wondered if they would make my child that night, but real children are made in silence, in the daytime.

All his trousers were too big. He looked like a scarecrow, but he didn't have straw hair. My mother fixed his belts by adding holes. His pants are like a long skirt cinched at the waist. He doesn't realize it, and we pretend not to notice.

He hasn't gone away forever or come back forever. He is here for another few hours, and I suspect he won't be able to come for my birthday, which falls on a Tuesday. That will mean one less gift for me, the gift of his presence. He won't be here for his own birthday either, which comes exactly one week after mine.

His mother called him. She probably talked to him about the Major, about her house in Florida, about walnut pies and her new car. My grandmother never talks about anything else. My mother did her best to make her understand that her son was in the hospital, but she carries on as if she doesn't hear. Hospitals are for the dead and for those who have lost an arm or a leg, she says, and since her son is neither dead nor a legless cripple, the hospital and his sickness don't exist. She might as well have said that her son doesn't exist. At least we'd have some peace.

On Sunday he would have liked it if we had all taken him back to the hospital. Mathilda, Anne, Gandhi, Ali, Monsieur Kowaleski, Irina and I. Come along, of course, we don't often get a chance to see each other. My mother said yes for the family, but for Mathilda and the Kowaleskis, she said that was too many. Anyway, there's not enough room in the car. The Kowaleskis left; Mathilde stayed in the house; and we went along with my father. It was a fine autumn afternoon, and when my mother parked the Volks to face the setting sun, our faces glowed red and our hair shone brightly. We were silent for a long time, Gandhi even stopped wagging his tail. Then my father turned around with his little boy's face, and he said, Good-bye, children.

They got out, and we waited for my mother till long after the sun had set. Ali peed on my slacks. In the hospital, my father cried in my mother's arms, then he tore the sheets that the nuns had ironed so carefully off his bed and threw them into the corner. And then he sat on them and said he wouldn't move until my mother came to get him next week. Orderlies arrived and gave him an injection—he who has never taken an aspirin in his life—and she stayed till he fell asleep, in the easy chair in his room, waiting for the nuns to come and make his bed. That night I kept my head under my bedside lamp for a long time.

~

At Christmas, we invited a lot of people from my mother's family whom I didn't know. On Christmas Day it was like a barracks after a general alarm. Mathilda had spent more than a week cooking up a feast for us before she went back to Uncle Aimard and Aunt Emma's for the holidays. When my mother isn't cooking, Mathilda takes care of everything. Actually, it's better if Mathilda does it.

She showed me how to make an apple poundcake and chicken with olives. Since we no longer eat steak at home because I nearly died we've been discovering Mathilda's talents. With some exceptions, cakes are still forbidden and the exception for the poundcake was for my birthday.

It was a carnival. Each family of cousins had brought a table and some folding chairs. They were all over the house, even in my bedroom, and everybody was shouting. The exchange of presents wasn't so much fun because of my cousin Simon. No one had thought to bring him a present. I realized I should always have a present in reserve for the person who is overlooked, even if that person is me.

My father recited a poem he had written. He's been writing poems since he stopped working at the factory. It was his Christmas present to me, to replace the gift of his presence at my birthday. *Then you are fully protected, O limpid, undulating fugitive, between the pure void and the extreme scintillation of day.* I repeat these lines before I go to bed. I repeat them ten, fifteen, a hundred times. "Fugitive" is the most beautiful word in the world. It is the reason I want to write music, so I can put "fugitive" into clear notes, into scales, arpeggios. Everyone applauded. Everyone knew that my father had spent months in the hospital, where he refused to sleep in his bed until my mother returned. Everyone is kind to him, and I am too, now that he no longer sends me to my room to finish my meals.

My aunts came with bags of clothing for the family because we're starting to be really poor, like the Commander's husband's workers, except that my father's not a worker, he's sick. Since my father stopped working at the factory, we buy only essentials. My mother sold her engagement ring. She sold it to the wife of one of the managers at the factory. We're eating the engagement ring just now. But nobody knows. Except for me.

I told my cousins the story about the great horned owl. If my mother hadn't been there to say it was true, they wouldn't have believed me. People believe only what they can see. We went tobogganing the day after Christmas. It had snowed all night, and we had permission to slide down the steep slope of the ravine. It was like jumping into space. My cousins shouted, Hoo, hoo! to frighten the owl and to tease me. I think that deep down they were very frightened themselves. They told me they thought it was the owl that had stolen the shoe and sock of the woman who jumped in the river.

I had never met my maternal cousins before this Christmas. There are no cousins on my father's side. Anne and I are the last of our generation to bear my father's name. If my mother doesn't act soon, there will be no one to pass on my father's name. That's why I wish I'd been a boy. So I could pass on his name to my children. They will never bear my father's name unless I marry him. Then any children I had would be my brothers. And I also want my children to be the children of a chef. For the time being, my favourite cousin is Simon, the one who was overlooked. I may write to him some day.

They've gone now, with their tables and folding chairs. They left after four days. That's a long time, four days, to sleep on the floor. They didn't see the great horned owl but they met Esther, Rajiv and Irina. They made fun of Rajiv's colour: he is very brown even in winter. I was relieved when they left. I couldn't wait for the return of Mathilda, who had promised me a bottle of Aunt Emma's raspberry syrup. We haven't gone back to the farm because since the summer Aunt Emma has been very sick. She has lost her long gray hair that she always put up on her head with combs in the morning before she went riding in the woods on Marianne.

Aunt Emma is going to die, my mother told me. Her disease is called cancer, and it's because of the minks and the products that have to be put in the cages to clean them whenever they replace a dead mink with a live one. At mealtimes Uncle Aimard won't have to listen for the slightest sound while he looks at Aunt Emma's empty chair. He will finally understand that the silence of the dead is much worse than the noise of the living.

My father came home in November, at the beginning of a strike by the factory workers. The factory bosses didn't want him there to talk to the workers, to say nothing of speaking in the workers' name. They told him, Stay at home, and that's all.

He makes me go over my lessons as do the fathers of most pupils in my class. We've never worked so well. I hope the strike will last a long time. I hope my father never goes back to work in that factory. My mother gives piano lessons, and Mathilda looks after Anne. Gandhi's coat is thicker because of the cold, and Ali gets into mischief with my mice. He ate some of them, and I thought my mother would discover the secret, with all the dead mouse heads strewn across the carpet. But my mother can't see very well, especially something lying around on the carpet. From now on I forbid Ali to go to the cellar. He'll have to be satisfied with Gandhi's tail and with the balls of scrunched-up paper I dangle on a string.

The morning after my cousins' departure, Anne gave herself a clown's face. My father has stowed a box of paint in tubes under the kitchen sink. On rainy days he paints on a big canvas fastened to his bedroom wall. Ever since my father came home from the hospital he has his own room. He paints, on the same canvas, the same shapes that look like upside-down mountains, and then when he's finished applying the colours he whitens the canvas and starts again. I don't know how he can sleep with the smell of paint. Even Gandhi can't stand it. Even me, though I like my father better since he's been home from the hospital, I need to go out and get some fresh air to keep from fainting. What happened was that very early on the morning after my cousins left, Anne crawled under the sink and opened a tube of red paint that smelled bad. It's my cousin Pascale's fault because she was rooting around all over the house for four days, as if it wasn't enough to root around in her nose. She mustn't have put the top back on the paint tube tightly enough. Anne ate some of the paint, she smeared it all over, on her pyjamas, in her hair, in her eyes, on her cheeks. A red ball drooling disgusting red liquid. I was the one who found her under the dining-room table. She was fainting because of the smell but she was still laughing. I woke up my mother, then I woke my father in his room. Gandhi started to moan when Anne fainted. We had to take her to the clinic to get cleaned out. They vacuumed her stomach and sponged her face. They threw out the pyjamas. Because of her red face my mother sometimes calls her Pompom. When she opened her eyes after her cleaning my mother said: Hello little Pompom, and Anne started to laugh. I'd rather see her laugh than fall into a big hole like Malou. My mother chucked out all my father's paint tubes, and the half-whitened canvas stayed on his bedroom wall until we moved to another house.

~

Irina came the other day with her brother Jan. It was the first time Jan had come to our house. He wants to take piano lessons with my mother. The piano is in the cellar, and Jan asked where the mice were. I was mad at Irina for not keeping her mouth shut. Actually, Rajiv is the one I should have been mad at, because I never told Irina about my family of mice. Rajiv was the one who told Irina, and she told her brother who almost got me in trouble. Now I know how careful you have to be about who you talk to. Esther wouldn't have said a word. My mother, who is always distracted, didn't hear a thing. I muttered, One more word out of you, pal, and I turn you in, and your mother will find out about all the dumb stunts you pull at school because I'll write and tell her. Jan is hopeless in school. He never writes to his mother. It would be strange for her to get a letter from me.

When he put his hands on the piano my mother fell silent. So did Irina and I. Jan at the piano isn't the same Jan who finds a million ways to harass his sister and pulls dumb stunts at school. My mother asks him where he learned that. At school. Now I understand: Jan is a poor student because he spends hours at the upright piano in the teachers' room instead of going to class. And the teachers don't say anything because at the piano Jan is transformed into a prodigy.

He plays so well my mother says there's nothing she can teach him. He reads all the notes and casually, just like that, he plays a Schubert Impromptu. I swear I'm going to write my first pages of music just for him. When he's finished he makes Irina promise not to say anything to Monsieur Kowaleski. My mother invited him to come every day if he wants. Jan never once came back to play in our cellar. He continues to find a million ways to harass his sister, and later he'll get into plenty of trouble when he plays the piano in bars to make his living.

~

We are poor. When the factory bosses told my father to stay at home and that's all, they meant forever. My mother went to tell them that with just her piano lessons and her engagement ring she would never be able to feed two children, a husband, a dog and a cat. The bosses said that's too bad. The bosses never say very much. Besides saving salaries they save words. For once, my mother didn't cry. She had brought Anne and me to the office of the most important boss, who called in all the other bosses to back him up and say: Forever. They looked like penguins in their suits and ties. If they'd been brave they would have told my mother to get rid of her whole tribe, especially my father and Mathilda. But they aren't brave so they let us go, wishing us good luck. Mathilda will stay at our house as long as Aunt Emma is alive. It's Aunt Emma who pays her wages. My father will stay too, as long as he's alive, even though he's not the one who pays Mathilda's wages.

We were just about to leave the factory when a deputy-boss came up to my mother and told her she'd have to give up the house. The house belongs to the factory, like the ravine, the river and the forest behind it. The factory owns the workers, too, and that's why they went back to work after Christmas. So that they could buy presents next Christmas. When we got back to the house my mother called my father's mother. She didn't give her time to talk about her pies and her jewels. Now my grandmother won't be able to say that she doesn't know my father spent months in the hospital or that there's no more work for him at the factory or that the house doesn't belong to us any more because it never did belong to us. And we'll need some of the Commander's legacy so that we can eat and send the children to school.

My mother must have got something because she told us the next day that our grandmother was giving us three months. Three months for my father's pills to take effect and for him to find work. My grandmother doesn't know there's just one factory in our town and in all the towns around us, and that the whole population works there unless they're musicians. And even then, the musicians work for the factory bosses when they order little concerts for their parties. My mother takes my grandmother's three months and asks each of her sisters for two more. I have to finish my school year. Afterwards, we'll find a way. I know that later on Aunt Emma will be dead, and we'll move away from this cursed town and leave behind Esther, Rajiv and Irina. Mathilda will go home to her father, who is Uncle Aimard's head farmhand, and she'll marry one of her cousins, as people in her family always do. My mother didn't cry but I did; I cried a lot, in secret, under the covers with the lamp lit above my face. It was the first time in my life I'd ever cried.

~

On the day we returned to the Commander's town, the old Volks gave up the ghost. Aunt Emma had done the same the day before we left. In my schoolbag were the Book, my notebook, a letter from Esther to be opened in my new bedroom, Marie Tamponnet's earrings and two mice. I left a supply of cheese and potatoes in the cellar in case the new tenants forget to feed them. Nothing here has changed; there is still just as much brick and asphalt. At last I'll be able to read some pages from the Book over Malou's hole. I'll take Anne with me, and when I'm tired of reading, we'll play ball.

I've decided to wear Marie Tamponnet's earrings. Before I even settle into my new room I take some ice cubes to freeze my earlobes. I make a hole in each lobe with a needle, and I don't feel a thing. There is no blood. I take the earrings that have been in their tissue paper all these years and put them in the holes. Now it hurts, and it takes all the courage I possess not to ask my mother to help me. When I'm finally able to pass the stems through the holes I'm very proud of myself. I finally look like a girl, a real one, and I have everything I need to be a whore. My mother doesn't notice. She doesn't notice anything nowadays. I hope she won't forget my birthday. There's plenty of time till then. That's what I tell myself for reassurance.

Here is Esther's letter. Dear Fanny, Our blood is mingled. With Rajiv's and Irina's too. The three musketeers have lost their d'Artagnan because it was your turn. We'll never know what happened to the shoe that belonged to the lady in the river. I'll never see Rajiv again. I'll never see Irina again. That's the way it is. I'll never have another friend to have silence contests with in the schoolyard during recess. I'll have to put up with noise, and I'll still have my dream of seeing you come back to my city as a missionary nun. I know you'll never be a missionary nun. There's no such thing as missionary nuns who are whores and who marry chefs. Don't write to me. Our mingled blood is enough. I'll go in the cellar window to get your mice, before the new tenants arrive. I'll take them to the river in the ravine and drown them. I love you. Esther.

I restrain myself from writing to tell her that in any case the mice wouldn't have made it through the winter.

We brought along the old Underwood when we moved. My father writes for a newspaper that doesn't pay him very well. He comes home late at night, and I hardly see him any more. In the morning he sleeps off his wine, my mother says. Sleeps off his wine between news assignments. That's what it means to be a journalist. You sleep off your wine between news assignments. He doesn't pick up Anne in his arms any more, but Anne still laughs. She can walk now. I should say, she dances. Three steps to the left, three steps to the right, then a pirouette. Her first shoes are ballet slippers.

We went to Malou's hole, Mama, Anne and I. The violet hadn't grown. I planted another, and we had a picnic with bread-and-mustard and fruit. My cousin Simon came. I hadn't forgotten him even though I never wrote to him. We lay down in the grass next to the hole, and he read *Rocambole* while I read the Book. Then we walked back home, and when we left him outside his house, he kissed me. It tasted like mustard, but I was glad. It made me feel as if I had to make peepee. When we got back to the house I tried to make peepee standing up, like Rajiv, and I got it all over the tile floor.

Outside his house Simon also asked me to come and read my Book in his room next Saturday. I told him I could come tomorrow, Monday, since I hadn't started school yet. He prefers Saturday because of summer school where he's taking remedial classes. I can't wait.

Wine is better than pills. Since my father has been sleeping off his wine—even though we don't see him very often because of his work—he doesn't seem as much like a scarecrow. I think he sleeps off his wine to forget the pills. My mother says it was well worth defending a thesis against capitalism so he could write stories about stray dogs. My mother always exaggerates. Anyway, since we've finished eating the engagement ring, my grandmother's three months and the two months from my mother's sisters, we've been eating my father's salary, the one he earns by the skin of his fingertips. There must be a lot of stray dogs in other countries because my father goes away a lot.

He takes the old Underwood with him, and he calls us every day. If he doesn't call, it's because it is too difficult. It was one of the bosses at the newspaper who persuaded him to leave the factory bosses' town and return to his home town to write about stray dogs.

While we wait for him, we've been decorating the new apartment. I left the drawing of the great horned owl on the wall of our other bedroom, so now I make a new drawing, for me this time. No great horned owl, the owl belongs to the other town. I draw a piano in memory of Jan, to whom my mother left her piano. Actually she left it to Monsieur Kowaleski because Jan had gone to his mother's village. He'll have a surprise when he returns. The keys of my piano are red and black, to be different. I put the colour directly on the wall so I won't be sorry not to be taking it when we move. I draw a staff under the piano, and some notes. It's my first composition.

The piano painted on the wall is enormous. At night it seems like the shadow of a Cyclops. I must sleep with my eyes open. I have my own room; Anne has her room; and my mother and father have theirs, with two beds in it. With two beds they won't be making a child for me.

Where we live there are lots of children my age who don't go to school. They don't go to school in the summer, which is normal, but they won't go in September either, because they don't know how to read. I feel sorry for them. Apparently they spend all day playing and yelling and whining with other children, in other words getting on the nerves of their mothers who have other things to do besides look after them. That's why I tell my mother that Anne has to go to school right away, so she won't get on my mother's nerves. When children get on their parents' nerves, it makes for bad parents.

Anne is a little young to start reading the Book with me, but she would be wonderful in a dancing school with her new ballet slippers. She would learn the writing of her body. She would teach us to read the lines of her body that is at once ethereal and dense.

One day she talked. It was the day of the gâteau Saint-Honoré. She was gabbing and gabbing, I don't know why, because in our family we're not very talkative. She talked about this and that, about the weather, about her childhood memories and her plans for the future. It was the day of her first birthday in May, in the factory bosses' town. We had more fun together than we'd ever had before. Counting Ali and Gandhi there were seven of us. Mathilda had baked some gâteaux Saint-Honoré. Not one, several! Dear Mathilda, I miss her so badly! One cake at the beginning, another in the middle and still another at the end. And wine. That was at the time when my father first started replacing his pills with wine. My mother said we'd get indigestion from eating so much cake, but nobody got sick.

It was a little because of me that we had the Saint-Honorés because I'd told Anne about the chef. What do you want for your birthday? Saint-Honorés. Yes but what else? Saint-Honorés, nothing but Saint-Honorés. She got them and so did we. Gandhi got some on his nose. By the end of the meal, Anne was dancing on the table. You'd have thought she had been drinking wine. While she danced she told us stories about her life. For instance, the day she dived into the river to get a piece of ice from the spring thaw. Gandhi brought her home by the skin of the diapers, soaking wet. My mother had always thought she'd got wet from watering herself with the garden hose so she'd grow faster. Or when she lit a whole box of matches in the cellar, next to my mice. We laughed about it, but she was punished the next day, which is absolutely unfair.

To decorate my new room, I ask for a mirror at the head of my bed. That way I'll be able to see the piano I've drawn on the wall even when I have my back to it. Lying flat on my stomach on my bed, facing the mirror, I read the Book, and I tinkle on the reflection of my piano. I can also scowl or smile at myself in the mirror, talk to myself and answer back.

I'm determined not to replace Esther, Rajiv and Irina. I shall be my one and only friend, my sole playmate for the mirror games. Simon can't be my friend because he's my cousin. I told the mirror when I came back from seeing Malou's hole that I couldn't wait for Saturday, that the number of hours to count till Saturday, and the minutes and the seconds, seemed like infinity to me. Infinity is long.

There is a space between the foot of my bed and the piano painted on the wall. My mother gave me permission to put the piano bench she hadn't given Jan Kowaleski there. You would almost think I was playing the painted piano. If I could, I would play tunes that tasted of the blood-red keys. In my room there are the window, the bedside table where I've stood the bedside lamp for the electricity that drives away dark thoughts, the mirror, the bed, the piano bench and the painted piano on the wall. And that's all.

My grandmother came back from Florida with numbered boxes full of plates, saucepans, glasses and cutlery that used to belong to the Commander and that she doesn't know what to do with. My mother thanks her, puts it all away in the cupboards and takes the old cracked plates down to the cellar. If they get stolen, too bad. Those plates are from the past and from unhappy recent memories of my father's sickness. Anyone who steals them will steal the unhappy memories, too.

My grandmother doesn't stay long; the Major is waiting for her downstairs. My mother had to bring up the nine numbered boxes because the Major's back is tired, and he's afraid of Gandhi. Ali dug his claws into my grandmother's legs. She's in a bad mood when she leaves, saying the apartment smells of cat pee. She's right; we never have time to change the litter. From my window I can see my grandmother shaking her head, which shows that she's worried about us.

In spite of everything she's the only one who noticed the holes in my ears and Marie Tamponnet's earrings. She winks at me and gently pinches my cheek. As she leaves she promises to send me some earrings.

~

Saturday comes, then Sunday. Simon wasn't there. He was playing football with some friends. The taste of mustard is bitter in my memory. Carrying my Book under my arm I went back to see Malou and the new violet I'd planted last week. I find the little silver spoon Anne had lost. My violet is wilted. For the first time I'm beginning to think that the Book wasn't meant to protect me from God, but to protect God from mankind. It has started to rain. It smells of wet earth because of the holes they've just filled. With my Book under my stomach I lie down on Malou's hole and try to take root there.

~

I took Anne and Gandhi over to Francine's. The Major came to get us so he could play real grandfather. We sat in the back, all three of us. He looked like the Commander's chauffeur. My mother gave me a rag to put under the dog, because of his hair, and a bottle of perfume for Francine. My mother wants a reconciliation with Francine. A conciliation, actually, because they've never been friends.

Francine has come home from London for good. She lost her future and her boyfriend, and now she is in her round bed, fasting, while she waits for another future and another boyfriend. We are there to entertain her. She doesn't ask any questions, and she doesn't listen to what we tell her. The afternoon unfolds in monologues interspersed with silence. Since she is fasting there's nothing for our afternoon snack. Gandhi chases her Abyssinian cat around the round bed. Francine asks me to lock the dog out on the balcony. I tell her he'll eat all her plants, but she pays no attention. She puts on some music, and Anne dances on the carpet. Francine has a big silver ring set with turquoises. When I die it will be yours. I don't want her to die because I don't like the ring.

The Major is waiting for us downstairs, really all he needs is the cap. He is in the car smoking and reading a newspaper that's not the one my father works for. When nap time comes, Francine splashes herself with perfume and gives me a book of poems for my mother, a necktie that used to belong to her boyfriend in London for my father, a pair of red ballet slippers for Anne and a carnival mask that she'd brought from Venice for me. It's a mask with feathers and sequins in the corners of the eyes. It's beautiful, and I put it on right away, to surprise the Major.

We pile into the back, and he tells me to be careful about dog hair. If he could only see the balls of dog hair under my bed he'd never let Gandhi get into his car that

86

reeks of cigarettes. He hasn't noticed the mask. And what if it wasn't me behind the mask?

He has an errand to do. I'm embarrassed because I forgot to make peepee and now I have to go badly. He stops at a service station. He orders us to get out and go and see if I'm there. That's what he says. Get out and go see if I'm there. He puts his car into a washing machine for cars. He could have waited and done his laundry later. You have ten minutes, and if you're not here in ten minutes, I'm leaving. Just like that, in the middle of nowhere. The Major can be very mean when he wants.

On the roof of a house I notice some bird droppings. I'll have to keep an eye out for those bird droppings if I don't want us to get lost. We leave: Anne, Gandhi, and I. Gandhi's leash stayed behind at Francine's, in the plant graveyard on her balcony. I only think of it now. Gandhi prances around, first in one direction, then another. We follow him, of course, so we won't lose him. We don't lose him, but we get lost ourselves. He runs fast. The streets are long, the houses tall. I counted the floors, there are at least fifteen. I'll never be able to find the roof of the house with the bird droppings.

I don't know how to calculate ten minutes. That's how many footsteps? How many houses? How many floors? How long till I wet my pants? Anne loses one of her red ballet slippers. She cries. Gandhi finds it in a shrub. Ten minutes had passed long ago. I know, because the sun is starting to set behind the buildings, and my pants are all wet. So I stop. Gandhi comes back, and we sit on the sidewalk with our feet in the road. Anne has dried her tears, I put the mask on her, and she rests her head on my shoulder.

Suddenly the big washed car drives up. Inside are my mother and Francine, with the leash and the dead plants in a box. The Major stops two centimetres from my feet, and my mother gets out of the car screaming. She hits me on the head, one hand then the other. She goes too far. Take that, and that and that you little birdbrain. Gandhi doesn't like it when anybody touches me. He growls, and the Major lets fly with a kick in the rear. I'm sure it's because of the hair. We've been looking for you for two hours! And what's this disguise all about? She pulls off the mask, and Anne starts crying again. I look at Francine, and I see that she's in the clouds. Fasting doesn't agree with her. Everybody home now, and you'll go without the Book till school starts! Aside from kicking Gandhi, the Major doesn't move a muscle. I feel like telling him, Go and see if I'm there. To punish him I ask Anne to let go and pee all over the back seat of his nice clean car. I pull out some of Gandhi's hair and spread it around. I don't ever want to see the Major again, or Francine when she's fasting.

My mother hasn't forgiven me for the Major's ten minutes, even though it's not my fault. And she doesn't forgive my father who comes home late from his news assignment. At the newspaper they tell her, that's the newspaper business. And what if the newspaper business is another woman? my mother yells into the telephone.

She doesn't talk to me at the table any more. She slams down the plates and cutlery. We'll have to bring the boxes back up from the cellar. Anne is smiling again, mainly because of Ali who just had babies. It turned out that Ali is a girl, so she can make babies grow inside her belly and then let them out through her little tube. One day she'll be an Ali Babushka. When I saw the baby cats I wondered if the father was Gandhi, because of the colour. Ali is black and Gandhi is blonde. The baby cats are black and blonde except for one that's grey. But apparently it would be impossible, probably because of the difference in size.

On the plates my mother slams onto the table there's steak and brown spinach again, to punish me. If Mathilda were there she'd be looking at my mother in amazement. I don't eat. I had told her I would never eat steak again. At night I steal some cheese from the fridge, for my mice who sleep at the back of the closet and for me. I nibble just like them. My two mice have never had baby mice. Maybe I caught two boy mice without realizing, or two girls, though that doesn't stop them from sleeping in each other's paws. If I keep eating cheese like this I'll end up in a closet like the mice.

What's most terrible is the banning of the Book. No Book, no sleep. And to crown everything my right ear has started to puff up. Marie Tamponnet's earring is stuck in the hole and it's impossible to get it out. I pull my hair over my ear. It gives me a funny look that my mother says is ridiculous. She doesn't see the hole in my left ear because her eyesight is failing. It's true that a hole without an earring is very small when you never give your child a hug.

I took the left earring and the mask out of the garbage where my mother had thrown them and put them under my bed with Gandhi's hairs. No danger of anyone finding them, Mathilda's not around to sweep there. The pain in my right ear is excruciating. The more time passes, the more my father keeps us waiting, the more silent my mother is—a heavy silence that makes the plates fly—the more it hurts. One morning it hurts me too much to get up. My ear is glued to the pillow. When I touch it, it hurts all the way to my back.

She finally came to my room to see what was keeping me glued to my bed. I don't want her to look under my hair. She gets so mad, I pray she'll go blind. When she lifts up the mass of hair she's horrified. Her anger is transformed into pity. She doesn't say anything about the earring that's buried in the swollen flesh. Only: you poor child, you poor child! Anne laughs because she was afraid of my mother's anger, too. This time I laugh till I cry, a straightforward laugh and dry tears.

The doctor came. He took out a long needle, finer than the one I used for the holes and stuck it into my backside. It feels as if the needle is going to find its way to my stomach, but I don't care; it doesn't hurt as much as my ear. You must apply compresses, Madame, he says, tugging at the earring. Hot compresses first to draw out the pus, aspirin, and I'll come every day to give her an injection. The pus can draw out whatever it wants, and take along the dark thoughts my lamp won't chase away! I ask her for Marie Tamponnet's earring and I slip it under my pillow, as if it were a tooth, hoping a fairy will leave a piece of fruit there tonight. I haven't eaten fruit for so long.

My father came home. That didn't help matters. I was still in bed, convalescing. My mother allows me to read the Book now, but I don't feel like it. She didn't say anything about the holes in my ears, just that we'll have to make a new one in my right ear because one hole is more vulgar than two. She comes every night to lay her hand on my forehead. The other night she heard the mice. I told her it was the floor. It creaks whenever it hasn't rained for three days. It rained yesterday, but there are exceptions. She believed me.

He came home late at night on the fourth day of my convalescence. I heard the key turn in the lock, very quietly, he didn't want to waken anyone. I wasn't asleep, that's why I heard him. He had pulled off his shoes, and he was walking on tiptoe. I called to him from my room. He came in and sat on my bed. He didn't want to turn on a light, but the moon was bright enough for him to see the compress on my ear. What happened to you? I made a hole in my ear, a hole like Malou's, and death was growing inside it, the doctor said. Death doesn't grow inside an ear, sweetheart, it grows in the soul, and as for the rest, we'll talk about it tomorrow. He smelled of wine, and I like that. A warm smell that comes through his white shirt. I asked him, Where were you? He replied, I was where the stray dogs are. I missed you, I tell him. Me, too.

My mother certainly didn't say that she'd missed him because he left again early the next day, before he even had time to kiss Anne good morning. He went to the newspaper, to settle some scores. They were looking for him, too. He came back right away, with a smile on his lips and a bottle of champagne in his hand. The scores had been settled, and his long absence earned him a scoop—I don't know which one, there were so many afterwards—and an extra half of a salary, too. This is for your trouble, he said to my mother as he uncorked the champagne. We didn't laugh because we knew what he meant: being somewhere else more often than here. Going away more often than coming home, if that's possible. We didn't laugh, but we drank his champagne, and he said nothing more about the holes in my ears. I didn't have the heart to reproach him for it. I got back into bed, and I brought along Anne and Gandhi. We shut the door, hoping the champagne would make bubbles in my mother's belly. I need that child they promised me, and I need the kind with the little tube outside, like my father's, otherwise I'll accept no further responsibility.

~

Children are the end of freedom, the beginning of slavery. That's how she told me her belly was inhabited again. In view of her enthusiasm, Anne and I didn't know if we should jump for joy or hope that it would pass. I went back to doing my homework on the dining-room table.

We kept one of Ali's cats. The others live with neighbours now, and we see them prowling the alley. The name of Ali's child is Nagrobis. He's the only one who looks like neither his mother nor Gandhi. He's all grey, and he never meows because he was born without vocal cords. He's a silent, inoffensive ball of fur who spends a lot of time in my closet with the mice. My mice won't last much longer. In their litter I find dried cheese they haven't eaten. I console myself with Nagrobis and my painted piano, on which I am making progress. My piano has no vocal cords either.

There are boys in my new school, and I am still the smallest. Simon walks part of the way with me, but I don't talk. He's the one who talks, to gain forgiveness for having played football that Saturday. He talks about his father who died three years ago, in Avignon. He talks about his mother, who is bringing up her five children by herself and whom he admires. I admire her, too. His mother is my mother's sister, who gave her two months in addition to the three from my grandmother. I don't know where we'd be today without her. He talks about my new hairstyle since the business with the ear full of pus. He thinks that short hair suits me very well. I don't tell him I cut it myself when my father went to another country again for another scoop.

One by one the curls fell from my head. One by one, Anne put them in an envelope that I tossed under the bed, along with the mask and Marie Tamponnet's earrings. My hair used to be very long. Very curly, very blonde, very everything a father can dream of for his daughter, but I cut it all off, to get revenge on my own father, as a matter of fact. I look like a naked caterpillar or like something the cat dragged in, to quote my mother who wouldn't let our neighbour finish the job. Our neighbour, Nicole, who lives on the same floor as we do, is a hairdresser and she changes her hairstyle every week. When she saw mine, with hair of every length, she wanted to fix it. My mother said no, that it would be a good lesson for the next time I do something stupid. Still, Nicole put her scissors to good use in exchange for one of Ali's cats, and now I have hair like a boy's. Nicole wouldn't make my hair red like hers, and the following week when I saw her new look, with yellow, curly hair, I decided she'd been right to refuse.

My mother cut off my eyelashes. She says that it used to be done quite commonly hundreds of years ago, the proof being Mona Lisa. I don't know who Mona Lisa is but I trust my mother's taste where eyelashes are concerned. She cut them short and Simon tells me it makes me look weird, especially when I frown. You look as if somebody plucked your head then singed you with a flame-thrower, is what he says. The eyelashes are supposed to grow back thicker and longer. They stayed short and straight, like combs with missing teeth.

At school they call me Stéphane because I didn't tell them about Fanny. It's still a secret between close friends and me, and there are never that many close friends. At the moment there are only Anne and Nicole. Francine has already forgotten, and since she is going on with her fasts, we don't speak. I still don't know if Simon deserves to be in on my secrets, about the placenta and all the rest. For the time being, he's the one who talks on our way to school, and I don't say anything. Not even about being plucked and singed.

On the way home, I'm always alone. Simon doesn't want his friends to see him with me. They don't know I'm his cousin. He doesn't tell anyone either. He's afraid they'll make fun of his family with my singed head and eyelashes. Luckily I do well in school. I do so well that I run off with all the prizes at the end of term, except the prize in religion that goes to the butcher's daughter who spends her whole life praying. That's because in religion the teacher and I don't agree, on account of the difference between his Book and mine. He is genuinely obsessed with God's son. I often have the same arguments at home, so I'm pig-headed, and the teacher doesn't like it. He gives me bad marks on all my assignments, which gets me excused from class after a few weeks, on the condition that I spend the class time in the office of the principal, whom I like and who asks me to correct her letters.

I'm still good at letters, even though I never send Esther the ones I write her. I mail the letters intended for her to myself. I am allowed two stamps a week. It's easy to pull the wool over my mother's eyes, especially since her sight is failing. I put my own name on the envelopes, imitating Esther's handwriting. My mother thinks she must have a lot to tell me since she writes so much. I read these letters to Anne, making her also think they're from Esther. It makes me feel important, so much correspondence, and gives me the impression that my life has a beginning and an end and that I am somewhere in between, with Esther and our mingled blood.

The other day I almost told the principal I didn't believe in God and that was why the religion teacher had sent me to the principal's office during his classes. But since it's not altogether true, I restrain myself. She is kind, and I wouldn't want to hurt her. What I would like very much, though, is to talk about believing in God because I wonder if when you believe in God, you must at all costs believe in his son. When I say believe in his son, it's as if I accept that God has a son but that I wasn't sure I believe in him. You can accept the existence of someone and still not necessarily believe in him. And I don't even believe in the existence of God's son. Where would God have found the time to have a son, to teach him to read and write and count, when he's already so busy teaching his people to love Him. And besides, God's son would need a mother, and anyone who says it's Mary doesn't know what they're talking about, because of her husband. God wouldn't have made a child with a woman who had a husband and who was born to a mother who was as much a virgin as she. All those complications are because of the business about the existence of God's son. If there hadn't been mankind to complicate the idea of God, God would be at peace today and so would I.

My principal wrote to her brother, who is a missionary in Africa. He must know the missionary sisters who came to my school when I was in the other town. When she runs out of things to write to him she asks me to add a few words, a page, for the missionary brother, to make the letter thicker and to make it worth putting stamps on the envelope. The first few times I write pages that are very academic, things like: what I learned in geometry today, the number of pupils in my class, which trees shed their leaves; trivial matters. The principal, who always re-reads her letters with my corrections and my little long-winded speeches to her brother, told me I could let myself go; I wasn't obliged to do as she did and fill a page with small talk.

The first time I let myself go, I wrote about Francine's fasts. The second time, about the Commander and the noxious smell. I asked him if that smell follows us all the way to the kingdom of God. It took an effort to write that letter. I didn't wait till he'd replied to tell him about my father's scoops and about Malou. He sent me a lengthy reply, reassuring me about the Commander's smell and telling me that now she must be in the odour of sanctity in the kingdom of God, with Malou and all the members of my family who are in holes. He also talked about God's son, who had been the subject of one of my letters, and about the spirit of God which is holy, and he told me I should drop those questions and turn my thoughts only to God. He added that he had trouble himself with God by way of the Son and the Holy Ghost, but I didn't understood.

My principal keeps the letters in a drawer. She doesn't want my mother to know that I'm corresponding with her missionary brother in Africa. Parents always get strange ideas in their heads, she said, especially yours.

~

So there's a boy in your belly, with a little tube like Papa's. I thought my saying that would reassure my mother. She shrugged and murmured that she could do without it. He will arrive in the spring, at the same time as the flowers on the magnolia in the garden that no longer belongs to the Commander because she's dead. He will be here in time for my father's return, one that only the new child will have waited for, inside my mother's belly.

When Nicole heard the news she wanted to celebrate

with sparkling wine. We told her that even if it wasn't champagne, it would bring back unhappy memories and that it would be better to think of something else. I gave her the recipe for Mathilda's apple poundcake and the three of us, Anne, Nicole and I, ate it; my mother didn't want any because she has nausea, real nausea from the child in her belly. Nicole's poundcake is almost as good as Mathilda's.

My mother saw the doctor that afternoon to check on how well he's attached. If the baby isn't properly attached I'll send him away. Send him where? To see Malou. I didn't know you could unattach children you don't want. But he's properly attached, and my mother decides to keep him.

I accompanied my mother to the doctor's in our new car that isn't new but that isn't as old as the Volks. It's big, and it smells of bread instead of dog. Apparently it used to belong to a baker, and when I get into his car, I feel as if I'm the soft part of the bread. The doctor's office has a big poster showing the inside of a belly before a child comes to live there, then the inside of a belly after the child is attached. All bellies are the same, so the first one is like mine and the second like my mother's. Inside, it looks something like the head of a goat with horns. What surprises me is the size before and the size after. I didn't know the insides of bellies are adjustable. There's a list of words with black lines joining them to an organ. Whoever thought up the Fallopian tubes was a creep.

The baby on the poster looks like a little Chinese child, or like Malou. When the consultation is finished I ask the doctor if every baby in the world looks like the one on the poster, with slanted eyes. He says yes. So does that mean that Chinese people are babies who come out before it's time, who come out before their eyes are straightened out? What about Malou? When I ask about children who are dark, like Rajiv, he has no answer. Perhaps it's a dye they add to the cord that attaches them to the placenta.

I'd like it if the son she is carrying could be called Esther. You asked me before and if I said no for Anne, I see no reason to say yes for this one, especially if it's a boy. Esther is a girl's name, and you don't give a girl's name to a boy. Yes, but you gave me a boy's name. Apparently it was different for me.

I write to my father in his scoop city where they're having a revolution. He won't be here with us for Christmas because he's the only one who would agree not to spend Christmas with his family so he could cover the revolution in the foreign city. He is in a city where they don't celebrate Christmas because of their religion. I didn't know that you celebrate Christmas because of religion. For me, Christmas is spending hours and hours at the window watching for a sleigh being drawn through the sky by reindeer. Christmas is pretending there's a chimney where the chief of Christmas throws down presents for good children. In our old house in Esther's city we had a fireplace, but last year I wasn't good enough to get anything except a sweater Simon's mother had knitted. That's a lot, but I'd have preferred a doll.

My letter to my father is just one page. A page that's actually a drawing with a caption. This is the belly of an unknown woman who has a baby with slanted eyes and black skin. He is a little black Chinese boy, and I don't want my brother to look like him. Do something and send your reply down the chimney that we don't have, but we can pretend that we do.

On Christmas Eve they delivered a huge cardboard box to us. Written on the top, the bottom, the sides, and even inside, was the word FRAGILE. The box is so big we'll make it into a house for Gandhi, Ali and Nagrobis; and I'll paint daisies on it so they'll feel as if they're in the country, in a meadow. Inside the box are a phonograph, some records and a bouquet of silk roses to stand in for a bouquet of real ones. It's nothing like the sort of table with a crank that scratched our Glenn Gould record; my mother now uses it for storing papers.

The men who delivered the box helped us position the phonograph in the living-room. It's too heavy for my mother and the baby. Even I can't budge it. We plug it in and it turns all by itself. The records my father sent are my mother's favourite music, all the Brandenburg Concertos, especially the Sixth. Anne dances with Gandhi and I say to myself, we're a happy family.

On Christmas Day there is a package at the door.

Inside the package are three little boxes: a gift for my mother, a gift for Anne and one for me. We open my mother's first. It's a long gold chain. It is wrapped around a white stone on a square of velvet. She puts the chain around her neck. It's very pretty, especially now that her breasts are heavier. Underneath the velvet square there's nothing, not a word or a name. Anne's box is tied up with ribbon. We have to cut the ribbon with scissors. Inside is a little swallow's nest with sanguine eggs. Three blood-red eggs that gleam. Aside from Anne's name on the gift-wrapping there's again nothing about whoever sent it. Finally I open mine. It's Francine's big silver ring with the turquoises.

She died on Christmas night after she'd left her package at our door. Since we have no chimney she left it on the landing. That wasn't very smart, somebody could have stolen it.

~

I give Gandhi something to eat. He's been hanging around the table for a while now, and it gets on my nerves. My mother is fat. She's worn out her wardrobe from the earlier pregnancies. I don't know what it is about this child in her belly, but he takes up a lot of room. He is spreading through my mother's body like a disease. He's everywhere, on her legs, her arms, her breasts. Just a few more weeks. Fortunately, because she can't take it any more. My father has left his revolution, to look after things.

Simon and his little sister Pascale have been invited to our house. I tried to befriend Pascale, but it didn't work out. Because of her plots against our family. Talking about us makes her feel important. On the subject of Francine, she told all our family secrets that were none of her business because Francine was my father's sister, and my father's family has nothing to do with hers. Some secrets she gave away, others she invented. Including some about the Commander's shameful disease that Francine might have caught, and my father too. That would explain the fasts and the electric shocks. That's all rubbish. The Commander's shameful disease couldn't be passed on just by talking. It would have had to be transmitted in the womb or the inside of her body. But Pascale likes spreading nonsense about everybody but herself. And that's why we aren't friends.

My mother was the one who invited her. I told her it would be our last attempt at reconciliation. I mostly look after Simon, whom I've finally forgiven, and Gandhi, who hovers around the table because he's so happy to see us all there together, a rare sight.

Pascale goes to the kitchen. I follow her to see what she's up to. My mother shouts to her from the dining-room: The juice is in the fridge. Pascale opens the fridge and takes out the juice. So far, so good. Gandhi has followed us; he wants some of my father's tarragon chicken that we've finished eating. The sauce is jelling in the dish, and my mother is keeping the bones to make stock. There's a little meat on the bones and that gets Gandhi excited. I want to cut him a piece, but I don't want my mother to know because I'm not allowed to touch the knife my father just sharpened.

I start talking to Pascale, just like that, tall tales, loud enough so they'll overhear but not suspect anything, on the other side of the wall, in the dining-room. The carving knife is really very sharp. If I were to mingle my blood with Pascale's I'd risk putting in too much. In the ship's kitchen the chef showed me how to proceed. Actually he didn't show me anything because he didn't think I'd be interested, but I observed, I saw how he slipped the blade into the flesh and with one confident stroke detached the meat, then put it on the plate.

I set Gandhi's dish on the counter, I go on talking about this and that, small talk. Pascale knows perfectly well that something's up and that I'm illicitly cutting some chicken for Gandhi who's not allowed to eat till we've all finished and the dishes are done. She tries to take the knife away from me. She grabs it by the handle. I say no. She says: Give it to me. I don't want to because once she has it she'll try to befriend my dog. She pulls as hard as she can, with all the strength of her meanness. I let go and the blade slices into me, very deep. I wonder if my thumb is still attached. It doesn't hurt. My father shouts: Is everything all right, girls? because I had let out a little yelp.

Pascale is livid, she's afraid of the blood that gushes out. I reply: I cut myself. Gandhi licks the blood off the floor, it's better than cold chicken. My father saunters into the kitchen. It's never serious when a child cuts herself. He sees Pascale, who is passing out, then the blood on the floor. A pool of blood. It still doesn't hurt. He takes my hand, looks at the wound; you can see the bone in the thumb, very white. This is serious, you have to see the doctor right away. They make me a tourniquet. I don't feel anything, I don't even sense the people around me. My father races to the hospital. He drives through red lights.

Nicole took Pascale and Simon back to their mother's in a taxi. My mother soothed Gandhi, who gets excited by the smell of blood, then she washed the kitchen floor. I spend the night on the operating table, with my father holding my other hand. The doctors find the severed nerves and tendons. They operate, plastic surgery they call it. The pain finally comes. They sew me up, twelve stitches, move my arm into a strange position for the plaster cast so the thumb can regain the strength to move, to hold a pen or paintbrush, to play the silent keyboard on my wall. It is my right hand. Like my piano keyboard, it will be silent for a long time. Pascale did a good job.

I stay out of school for several weeks. I spend that time in the hospital, and I ask that nobody come to see me. I have nothing to say to them. A lady turns the pages of the Book for me.

After the operation I have trouble walking. Though I didn't cut my foot. My head spins. When I can finally stand by myself I go to visit Noah in a dark room that smells of overcooked meat. Noah has burns over his whole body, and all that's left of his face is his eyes. Whenever I go to his room I have to wear a mask and gloves and special pyjamas. There are degrees of burns. That's something I have learned in the hospital. The third degree is the worst. It's the one Noah has, and the doctors don't hold out much hope for him.

I talk softly to him; only his eyes answer me. Planted in his two arms like stems of roses in black earth are very long, very fine tubes that let in water. They found Noah in his bed after his house had burned down. All that is left of his parents is a pile of ashes. The nurse told me. Now they're trying to find his father's sister, who lives far away, to come and talk to Noah. When I leave the hospital, I'll be surprised to see that she is as black as Noah. Even though she wasn't in the house that burned down.

Pascale is saying I attacked her. I don't contradict her. There is no defence against stupidity. You simply avoid it. So I avoid Pascale and anyone who believes her story. I have explained what happened to Noah, but my cut and my problems with Pascale are very insignificant next to his body that's like a big lump of coal. If I still had my placenta I would stick pieces of it on his face so I could see what he looks like.

The cast stayed on for four weeks. Long enough for

my mother to finish her baby, minus a few days. I went back to school in spite of the cast. Everybody wants to write their names on it. I refuse. The only names will be the principal's, Anne's (she drew a flower above her name which I wrote myself with my left hand) and my mother and father's because you have to. I listen to my teacher, and I'm exempted from compositions. When they take off the cast I'll have to learn how to write again. So I'll have trouble with it all my life! If Esther were here she would know what to do.

The boy arrived with the spring. It was already hot. Already the streets were spitting up the dirty papers that people had dropped there in the fall, now swirling in the wind. Spring is dirty papers that swirl through the streets before the buds come out. My city is dirty, and it smells of stagnant water. I will never get used to that smell, or to the noises that you can't protect yourself from. My room is noisy with the sound of motors running, of fans rumbling, of neighbours fighting. The walls are cardboard, the windows rags; nothing stops the noise. Only Glenn Gould and the Brandenburg Concertos bring me peace.

I feel sorry for the boy who is born into such a shambles. Anne and I were spared. As for Malou, I don't know. I do know that she wouldn't have put up with the greasy smell of frying potatoes that travels across the street and settles on the walls of my bedroom. It gives my piano a fine patina, a patina that stinks. If only they fried their potatoes with lavender or thyme, but lavender and thyme don't grow here in my country.

As I'd predicted, based on my mother's condition, the boy is enormous. He is the enormous pride of my parents who had to wait for one dead child and two girls before they saw that little tube. Finding a name for him is no small matter. Since I'm single-minded I suggest Esther, but my mother is single-minded too. She refuses. My cast has just been removed, and I can feel her refusal in every one of my stitches.

Now it is Anne's turn to give her opinion about the name. Anne only talks in one-word sentences. She began doing that when we moved. Those words don't always designate the thing, so you have to proceed by deduction. Now that my father has come home, Anne dances, draws, sings and reads; and she writes words as well as writing with her body. But she no longer talks as she used to, for instance, on her birthday with all the gâteaux Saint-Honorés. For thank you, she says flower. For Fanny, she says thanks. To say mama or papa, she says Annapurna, indiscriminately. For the boy, she says It'saboy. My parents don't like it, but for Anne and me, the name sticks, because it's the one that best suits him. Better than Henri, which is the name of the Commander's husband, that thief who passed on a shameful disease to his wife. It'saboy is a big boy with a big tube and a big appetite. Fortunately my mother's breasts are enormous, he'll be able to suck them all he wants before she deflates them.

I'd like to find that bastard who is wearing my placenta on his body. To show him my mutilated hand and yell at him, Teach me how to write! I can't even carry It'saboy in my arms, I can't write words without dripping onto the paper, without trembling, without worrying no one will be able to read me.

The principal is kind. I dictate my letters to her missionary brother, and she doesn't censor a thing. I correct her letters aloud, and I spend a lot of time in her office because these days she writes to him often. I tell her about my family, and she tells me about her brother who never comes to visit her.

When she sees my mutilated hand, she tells me that one day her entire body was one big sore. It was to defy an authoritarian aunt who had ordered her to stay away from the bushes because of a poisonous plant that burns your skin and isn't nettles. Sumach, she remembers. That's a pretty word. To prove to herself that her aunt's sumach didn't frighten her, she rolled around in the dangerous plant. I would never have done that. I'd have thrown the aunt into the sumach. In any event, the aunt went away, and my principal was very proud of her daring. A week later her whole body was one purulent blister and they had to suspend her in a hammock and then wipe up the water-filled pustules. She nearly died. I'm not going to die because of one oozing thumb.

My thumb is giving off a thick yellowish liquid. It is the ink I'll write with later on. I have to wrap my hand in a cotton bandage every night, then start again every morning. It's ugly, and it will always be ugly, says my mother. I keep my hand curled up on my stomach, from shame, and I clutch my handkerchief very tightly, like someone who is secretly crying. It will be this way for months, for the months until Anne's birthday, until my own and even till It'saboy's birthday next year, when beads will stand out on my thumb for the last time. In the meantime I suffer.

My mice are dead. Ali and Nagrobis polished them off in short order. So that's that. They sleep on the mouse litter in my bedroom closet. There's not enough room in the house so It'saboy sleeps with me. To make room for him my mother threw out the piano bench and now I have to play standing up. To keep from waking my brother at night, I have my sessions with the lamp in the closet, along with Ali and Nagrobis who also take advantage of the electricity to drive away dark thoughts. Sometimes I fall asleep there, with the cats on my stomach, the light in my eyes and my mouth wide open. It'saboy wakes me by howling, and I barely have time to slip between the cold sheets before my mother arrives. Anne would have liked It'saboy to sleep in her bed. Those two are already living a genuine love story. Apparently boys aren't supposed to sleep with girls before they're married.

I hold my pencil between my index finger and middle finger, otherwise it hurts. I can't bend my thumb. Putting on gloves or a coat is a big production. I've got used to holding my fork in my left hand, and I don't protest when my mother cuts up the meat on my plate. With fruit and vegetables I can manage on my own. There hasn't been a gâteau Saint-Honoré since Anne's birthday in the other city.

~

Since my father is at home between news stories, he cooks Chinese dishes, and he often takes me with him to Chinatown to show me lacquered ducks hanging by one foot. The pigs' feet floating in a thick sauce on top of the counter are disgusting.

Chinatown is the only neighbourhood that doesn't smell of french fries. It smells of shrimp so I feel as if I'm at the seashore. My father knows all the merchants and all the people who live in the neighbourhood. One day we go into a house that's not a grocery store. The stairs take us up to a room that's the first in a series of rooms that run the length of a corridor with mildew growing on the walls. Lying on mats and smoking a long pipe are a number of men and a few women who nod vaguely at my father. We walk through all the rooms, which are separated by red velvet curtains. I ask him if it's a hospital. He says, In a sense. If it's a hospital in a sense, is it a hospital some people wouldn't want anything to do with, where mama wouldn't want you to come? He doesn't need to make me promise not to say anything.

In the last room, a tiny little man is sitting in a huge armchair, so huge his legs don't touch the floor. He is sipping a brackish liquid, and he's grinning from ear to ear. My daughter, Stéphane. Introductions are made. Months later when I ask my father the man's name, he will tell me there was no man in the room and no room at all.

The conversation takes place in a language I don't know. The man keeps smiling while he sips his mixture. My father talks a lot, the man not much. He shows agreement by nodding his head, and he tosses in a word here and there in the midst of the continuous wave of words. As we are about to leave my father hands him a big envelope, and the man slips it nimbly into a drawer. He gets up, or rather he jumps out of his chair to show us to the door. He is barely taller than I am. He is a good ten times older than I am and at least twice as old as my father. You look like old Henri, he says as he embraces me, but in your eyes, there is sadness. You have eyes that do not know how to do wrong. Thank you for coming with your father. The man has bad breath.

In the car my father talks. Do you know what opium is? No. That's what you saw; it was what my grandfather's life was like after the Great War, and the man you met was his son. Are there great wars and little wars, Papa? My grandfather made that son with a Chinese woman from the neighbourhood. The man runs the biggest opium network on the continent. I see. My grandfather often used to bring me here with him. I see. I didn't love my grandfather, but I loved his son, the gentleman you saw there, even more than my mother. I gave him his father's diary, the one he kept for ten years before he died. On every page there is a reference to that son, who is the only child he really loved. When my grandfather died Francine inherited the diary. I just found it among her things. We'll never see that man again. Why? Because death always takes from the living the person she inhabits.

~

I get word about Rajiv and Irina. In a letter full of spelling mistakes Irina says that Rajiv broke his leg because his little sister tripped him. Aside from that, the usual banalities.

I've stopped counting the months and soon the years that separate us from the lady in the river. Nothing at all about Esther. I expected that; Esther always keeps her word.

Irina will go to see her mother next summer even though it's not her turn. Her two older brothers aren't going, they will work at the factory to help Monsieur Kowaleski who has cut himself again, his whole hand this time. Jan is still getting bad marks and playing the piano. They built a bench of the right size for him, and he is giving a concert in June. If we could come, it would make Irina very happy.

I'd like to attend Jan's concert. Esther would be amazed to see that I haven't become a missionary nun. Perhaps she got married? I could go back to the river, play d'Artagnan, kiss Rajiv now that I know how, say hello to Marianne and Cybèle, hold Mathilda in my arms.

I show my mother the letter. She just says, It's full of mistakes. That means we won't go. If she had wanted to, she'd have said, How would you like to go to Jan's concert? I hold the pen between my index finger and my middle finger and I write, Dear Irina, We won't be coming, Farewell, Fanny. The words are still poorly formed, but that's just too bad. I have no choice; I must write if I want to erase that part of my life.

~

Francine could have thrown herself into the river and left a shoe on the shore like the river lady, but the water is too cold at Christmas. She must have been afraid of being found disfigured, swollen, unrecognizable; she who took such good care of herself. She swallowed pills one at a time until fatigue overcame her, and she no longer had the strength to do anything but wait for the end.

They found her in her round bed, with the Abyssinian cat inside a bird-cage at her feet. I had sounded the alarm because of my ring. My father came back for a few hours. I mean, we saw him at the house for a few hours; he spent the rest of the time on formalities and in his dead sister's bed. The corpse had been taken away, of course. He's not the kind to sleep with a dead woman. He loved her as much as his grandfather's illegitimate son. With a love that cries out for silence.

I didn't want her cat because of Gandhi. He may be dead now, too. It was our second farewell ceremony between Christmas and the New Year. This one was grandiose. Friends came from all over. Francine was burned just as the Commander had been, and I watched the coffin disappear into the fiery hole with its bronze handles and all the flowers that burn along with the corpse. Unbearable. It was what she wanted. She wanted nothing to be left but a little heap of grey and white bones veined in red, where the blood had stuck.

They gave us the little heap in a black box, and I touched it. The lid wasn't sealed so I rubbed some powdered bones between my fingers. A burned body doesn't weigh much. I saw Francine in crumbs, and I discovered that death has a taste of salt when the earth has not done its work. A girl sang, and my grandmother cried. My mother inherited a pile of dresses. The phonograph didn't turn for weeks, and I swore I would never fast as long as I lived.

It'saboy has a weakness for my mother's right breast. Her left breast is flat and the right one leaks as soon as It'saboy cries. My hand leaks, too. I observe the two of them: she sitting in the wing chair, he clutching at life. Absolutely different from Malou. He has an athlete's feet, and Anne has the feet of a dancer. An athlete's feet that he flutters to ask for my mother's warm milk and her generous hand. For this time her hand is generous. She searches It'saboy's body; she explores, measures, grades, loves. And It'saboy drinks greedily, without let-up; even in his sleep he takes it in. He eats the air, he devours the night, he digests his dreams, while I, I don't sleep, I watch him, listen to him, admire him.

Since he was born my father has not returned to a country in revolution. The newspaper can wait. Between the Underwood and the wine, he tells It'saboy the story of his life. He tells him everything he has never been able to say since he's been old enough to talk, and I think to myself that a newborn is a lot better than electric shocks. He tells him about the good and the bad, the dark thoughts and Monsieur Kowaleski's amputated finger. It'saboy gurgles, he digests my father's words. As for me, those words go inside me like steak. I wish I could position myself between the two of them, three if I count my mother, and protect the child from their loquacity, protect him from their love that won't endure. On the matter of his pleasure, his little tube is eloquent.

Anne takes me dancing, holding my left hand. She takes me to dance on Malou's hole, and I sing. Birds have overrun the cemetery. They sing and dance with us. I find a dead dog just beside the tallest tree. His swollen belly looks up at the sky. I'm not afraid of dead dogs; there are plenty of them in my city. But that round belly stretched by the heat frightens me. What if there was room for a family inside? I don't want to leave it there. We have to find a hole like Malou's for the dead dog and its family.

With my foot I nudge it to the stream. I've taken off my sandals and now I'm in water up to my ankles. It feels cool. I wash the dead dog. At least this one won't go up in smoke. An animal is watching us, a big one, bigger than the dead dog. It sticks its head out of its hole and its whiskers twitch at the tip of its snout. I push the dog in its direction. The animal can take the dog into its hole and do its work. It's better that way, better than drying up under a tree while waiting for the crows to come and peck at its stomach.

On the way home I run into my father who is pushing It'saboy in his carriage. He is going to Malou's hole, too. He seems to be annoyed at seeing us. Annoyed at running into his daughters who went to dance and sing for Malou, as if we had something to hide from him. Anne wants to go back and dance and sing for It'saboy.

I stay by myself with the shouting children three streets away from my house. For once I want to join them and yell loud enough for my mother to hear me from her bed. I want my yells to disturb her afternoon nap. But I don't know how to yell, so I show the children my mutilated hand. I unwind the cotton bandage that I soiled with the dead dog. As I unwind it, it pulls. The wound is still oozing. The doctor said I needed a skin graft but my mother wants to let nature do its work, as she always says. It was by letting nature do its work that she killed Malou.

One more turn and my hand is free. The children yell even louder. I want to strangle them when they call me the monster. I wish their yelling were addressed to Pascale and Simon, to Irina, Rajiv, Esther, to Malou, It'saboy, Francine, the Commander, to my mother and father and the principal's brother who hasn't written to me since I cut my hand. Let them yell, the whole lot of them, and Anne and I will go to heaven without them.

I gather up the bandage and put it back every which way, with all the dust and dirt the rain hasn't washed away. I go home, leaving behind the children who are insulting me and calling me the monster.

Ali and Nagrobis are billing and cooing in my bedroom closet. They leave a little bit of room for me in the midst of the mountain of socks that have been lying there since the birth of It'saboy. I refuse to wash them. I'm disturbing Ali and Nagrobis. They kick me out of my closet. I need a dark corner though; I need to turn my attention back to my hand. Why all this sorrow and pain? My marks won me prizes and honours. Anne is making progress in reading, and she can repeat all the words in the first sentence of the Book. Her writing gets better and better. It'saboy is cutting his first teeth; soon he'll be able to eat my mother's breast. So it's not that. My sorrow is indefinable; it resembles my parents' spatters. It does not disappear in the lamplight. My sorrow is infinitely complicated.

I crawl under my bed where the dust creates a kind of nest for me. I find Marie Tamponnet's earrings, Francine's ring and her feathered mask. By blowing a little, by rubbing a little, I restore the earrings' shine. I wish I could wear them, along with the mask and the ring, but it's hard to find the hole with a mutilated hand and besides, I'm sleepy. If I could, I would sleep until the next time my father goes away.

They found me that evening. Actually it was the commotion in the apartment that wakened me. Gandhi was making an incredible racket in the bedroom. They had combed the neighbourhood, questioned all the bad children, searched the restaurant that sells french fries, rung the bell at Nicole's who has done stupid pranks with little girls before. It'saboy was howling with hunger when my mother finally unbuttoned her blouse and gave him a breast that was as swollen as the dead dog's belly. She did that after she'd scolded me, washed me and wrapped my hand in clean bandages. She also cleaned the dust from under my bed and threw out all the socks in my closet. Ali and Nagrobis hid under my blankets. I was punished for trying to hide my sorrow. I hate my sorrow and my mother.

The house on the lake is hidden by brushwood. My father had promised us a house for the summer, with a lake and a forest. He hadn't said anything about brushwood, and I didn't want to be poisoned by sumach lying on the paths. When it rains there are a lot of mosquitoes. I watch them take my blood and then I crush them. It makes a red flower on my arm.

I'm allowed to swim as long as I don't go too far away. Simon and Pascale are here. They sleep in the attic above my head. I swim alone, with Gandhi who remembers the good old days at Uncle Aimard's and Aunt Emma's. Anne is learning the breast-stroke; she dances with her arms.

The lake water should heal my hand. It will start to look like a hand if I do my exercises. I concentrate on opening and closing my fingers as if I were catching fish. I have four fingers that work. That's enough for the time being. While It'saboy splashes around inside his rubber ring, I go mushroom hunting with Anne. Simon and Pascale are fishing near the low wall. Fishing for raspberries for tonight.

I'm not angry with Pascale any more. No one believed her story, and she gave me a big notebook where I do writing exercises. On the first page she wrote: "To my cousin Stéphane, Pascale," with three Xs which means three kisses. That's better than one.

Anne finds some Russulas, and Gandhi brings us a

hare with a broken leg. Simon wants to cook it, but we tell him you don't cook an injured animal that hasn't died yet. He makes a face, as usual.

My father stays in town because my mother doesn't want his friends from the newspaper with their cards and bottles of wine to come to the lake. I wish my father had taught me how to gamble and drink every night. Sometimes he lets me light his cigarettes and besides making me dizzy, it reminds me of the cigars the captain and my chef used to smoke. I wonder how his little girl Aglaé is and if she still wears polka-dot dresses.

There's not so much work at the newspaper now, and the journalists play cards while they wait for something to come up. My mother doesn't like these friends of my father's. She refuses to leave her room when they're around, and my father has to bring It'saboy to her in bed so she can nurse him. Since my father started smoking, they've been waging a cold war, a territorial war, which my mother wins a little more each day. It started with the bedroom. She didn't want Francine's dresses to smell of tobacco, even though they already smell of tobacco because Francine was a smoker. My father slept in the living-room for weeks while he waited for the storm to abate. Then he went back to the bedroom and to his little bed beside my mother's big one. They exchanged the two medium beds for one little bed and a big one because of It'saboy, who takes up a lot of room. Afterwards, during their war, she won the dining-room and the kitchen, because smoke clings to food. Even though it's nothing compared with the smell of frying. Finally, she banned smoking in our bedrooms. Now when he comes in to give me a kiss while his friends are around the card table in the living room, he hides his cigarette, and I throw my window wide open. I ask him to give me a smoky kiss, and I lick from his lips the taste of the wine he has started to drink. All that are left to him are the living-room and the landing. The living-room on condition that the door to the balcony is wide open like my window. One night it rained into the living room, and my mother was furious. She couldn't say anything because she was the one who had asked that the door be left open.

~

The verandah floor isn't very solid. It'saboy nearly fell through the rotten boards last night when my mother was holding him. So my mother nearly fell too. There was more fear than harm done, but now we're not allowed on the verandah till they decide if they're going to repair it. For the time being, we have to go outside through the kitchen, walk around the house through the weeds, and then take the path to the beach. There's always a garter snake slithering through the grass when we go by, and it makes us jump.

We have pretty straw hats to protect us from the sun. Mine is red, yellow, green and black. My grandmother gave it to me, and I wear it all the time, even when it rains. Anne makes a fuss when she has to wear hers, which she thinks is too big for her and not as pretty. If I'm in a good mood, I lend her mine. I have to keep an eye on her; my mother asked me to. She could have a sunstroke, and to get to the doctor, you have to walk many kilometres to the village.

My father kept the car in case he wanted to pay us an impromptu visit. The baker comes three times a week with bread, pies and doughnuts. The milkman comes every day. For everything else we rely on my father's impromptu visits. Unless my mother is at the beach, we're not allowed to swim. We can dip our feet in the water or build sand-castles or sunbathe. It's silly; I'm a better swimmer than she is, and making sand castles is no fun at all. Most often we play ball and fish for crayfish. At night the bathtub is full of crayfish that my mother throws into a broth. She calls the dish swimming crayfish, but she never eats any because it gives It'saboy pimples through her milk, she says. The real reason is that she's afraid the crayfish will eat her stomach.

As for the raspberries caught by Simon and Pascale, I'm the one who deals with them. I made a raspberry pound cake by substituting raspberries for the apples in Mathilda's recipe. You just have to add a little extra flour.

I fell into the hole in the rotten boards that need to be replaced. I should have thought about it. I went to let in Gandhi who was scratching at the door, but I forgot the orders and ran through the house and the next thing I knew I was in the hole. Like Malou. I managed to get back on my feet by myself despite a skinned elbow, nothing serious.

The hole is the cave of Ali Baba and the forty thieves. A room full of trunks and armoires, books and pictures. We weren't allowed to go there. The owner of the house on the lake had boarded up the door to the cellar. It was my father who made the arrangements with the owner; the rest of us have never laid eyes on her. We'd looked for the keys to the two bolts on the door that was always shut, but they were nowhere to be found, and a fine wire mesh made it impossible to get access through the windows.

I thank God for my fall, and I grope around for a light switch. I find it behind the biggest armoire. Of course the bulb is burnt out or perhaps there isn't even a bulb. I can see Gandhi on the other side of the window getting worked-up and scratching at the ground. I have to find a way out, and I don't want to alert my mother. It would be hazardous to go up through the opening in the rotten planks. I could break my neck. For the time being, what I'm interested in is spread out before my eyes as they slowly get used to the dimness.

I'm afraid of finding a corpse in the biggest armoire, of smelling the noxious odour again. I pinch my nose and turn the key that's hanging from the lock. There is no corpse, only dresses, costume jewelry, satin, velvet, ribbons and feathers. Countless pairs of shoes on a rack seem to be waiting for a dancer's foot. It's a shame Anne can't see them. The small armoire is full of hats in boxes.

I open the lock on a trunk. It doesn't resist the claw of a hammer I found in a corner with the gardening tools we'll use to clean up the vegetable garden now lying fallow. I'll talk to my mother about it, and she'll talk to my father, who will talk about it to the owner of the house, whom we don't know. Perhaps she'll let us have the keys. In the trunk there are piles of old photos, newspaper clippings and letters that look like drawings. It's too dark to decipher them. I'll take the letters and photos to my room once I find a way to get out of here. I'll show them to Anne, and she will be able to tell me where these strange drawings come from. Anne knows things like that. I won't talk to anyone else about them, especially not to Simon who would be only too happy to go and tell my mother everything.

The visit has lasted long enough. I have to go up now before Gandhi barks and alerts the whole house. A short staircase leads to a second door that opens onto the lake side of the house. If I'm not mistaken there's a wall covered with ivy, which would explain why we've never noticed that door. The latch barely holds on the door frame. A single push from outside would have opened it. I clutch my package of photos and letters. The door does open onto the ivy-covered wall. I have trouble getting out and it's Gandhi who shows me the way. I've forgotten to close the door but too bad.

~

It's Chinese. She is categorical. I give her a brush, and she reproduces a sign, then two, and finally a whole row of signs identical to those on one of the envelopes. It looks nice, like a row of little soldiers in tutus. If it is Chinese, I'll have to go to Chinatown and see the illegitimate son of the Commander's husband and have him translate the row of little soldiers for me. I'll bring him Anne's sheet of paper with her drawings so as not to arouse suspicions. Her hunches are always right. When I look at the photos, I see faces with slanting eyes. The paper is yellowed. I stow everything in one of my drawers.

They've replaced the rotten boards, and I've returned many times to Ali Baba's cave, going through the door behind the curtain of ivy. I brought Anne along; she steps between the trunks like a cat. We even found a family of mice, and now they wait for us to bring them cheese. One day I got dressed up in a feathered hat, with a boa around my neck and a dress that was so long I nearly tripped. I'd unearthed a cigarette holder, and I lit up a little piece of driftwood. It was good.

Anne is fascinated by the pictures. There is one in particular that she'd like to reproduce, a certain Countess d'Haussonville. We have to persuade my mother to buy her some tubes of paint like the one she swallowed when she was little. Her resistance exhausted, my mother passes on the order to my father; it makes him smile. He remembers the half-blank canvas in his bedroom in the other town. What does she need paint for? To paint, and some canvas too, Papa, please. He brings an easel as well and asks to see her first creation. Not till it's finished. Not till the end of our holidays; not till we leave this house on the lake that belongs to an unknown landlady.

She spends hours, whole days in Ali Baba's cave by the light of an oil lamp. I invent barren harvests in the forest, crayfish hunts on rainy days. We no longer go to the beach. I have become the guardian of her inspiration, the one who is allowed to see what is invisible.

Simon and Pascale have gone. It was time, they were starting to lurk around near the ivy. I told my mother I'd skinned my elbow when I tripped on the path to the beach. It'saboy bit me, and I had a bout of fever plus a whole day in bed. Anne stayed by my side, reading. I knew it was her way of reading to me, in silence, to respect my fever, just as I play the piano standing up, in silence, on the red and black keys on my bedroom wall.

Anne is a great artist, a greater artist than Malou would have been if she weren't in a hole today. As for It'saboy, he will become a great athlete, because of his feet and his constitution, which is very strong from crying himself hoarse for my mother's swollen right breast. But my parents are just parents, neither artists nor athletes. As for me, I am mutilated. And that's my family.

We resume the reproduction sessions. I've unearthed a stool high enough so Anne can be comfortable when her canvas is on the easel. She gets on and off the stool like a gazelle when she wants to judge distance or perspective. The work is progressing. She often asks me to be quiet when I make too much noise turning the pages of the Book. I don't move. She mustn't be disturbed. Her work is beginning to make her look like the countess: the face almost perfectly oval, the smooth white forehead, the lip that casts a shadow on the chin, even her finger resting nonchalantly at the base of her neck when she is hesitating over what brush to use or what curve to draw.

Anne is being transformed; she is growing with every stroke of the brush. She is the reflection of her subject. I don't know how she manages to reproduce the shimmering of the dress and the countless folds that fall onto the hips, but the dazzling sight forces me into the silence she demands. Only the blue creates a problem. She cannot find the appropriate shade. Are our colours no good, or is it the light?

My mother doesn't suspect a thing; she's too busy making It'saboy love her. Gandhi is allowed to come inside now. He noses around everywhere. If the owner of the house on the lake has children, and if they are allowed to play in the cave of Ali Baba and the forty thieves, those children must be very happy.

Besides the paintings, hats, shoes, dresses, furs, photos, letters and newspapers, we find a small chest filled with jewels that must be false, because no one would leave so much gold, so many precious stones at the mercy of our curiosity. There are hundreds of bouquets of dried flowers hanging by their stems, books, a cardboard box filled with glasses of every colour, silver ewers on an étagère, two globes, a sextant, a crystal ball, an old bathtub, pens, pen-holders, inkwells and reams of yellowed paper that I use to make airplanes. When Gandhi is with us, Anne can't work, so then we explore. We dress in court clothing for afternoon tea, and we push the easel into a corner.

One morning a wasp stings Anne on the lip. She also has a lot of bites on her arms, but it's the one on the lip that is dangerous, the village pharmacist tells us. She stopped breathing for a few seconds, and I was afraid my dancer would never dance again. It is It'saboy's fault: he howls at the top of his lungs, and he flings his toys all over as soon as my mother goes away. I get upset and tell him to be quiet. When I get upset, Anne does, too, and she runs around in every direction at once. I knew there was a wasps' nest near the hollyhocks. Simon was going to burn it, but he forgot.

She went running towards the nest because she was excited, and she stepped on it. The wasps got angry.

Luckily we were all wearing socks and long pants that day because it gets cool quite early now, so her dancer's legs and feet were spared. The wasps attacked my fingertips three times, three stings that made me forget my mutilated hand, the hole in my ear and my other little woes. Anne was stung a dozen times, and her pain was a hundred times worse than mine! We daubed mud on her arms, but her lip was a problem. The milkman told the doctor who told the drugstore to send a syringe and some liquid to inject in her buttock. Her whole body was swollen, and I was afraid that the syringe would make her burst like a balloon and that we'd find pieces of her all over. The injection relieved her, and she fell asleep, smiling like an angel as she always does, while I glared at It'saboy. The next day, of course, she forgave him for everything. She played with him: I tickle your chin, and you tickle my chin and the last one to laugh is the winner. She was always the one who lost.

It's a masterpiece! We waited till everyone was asleep, then we brought the painting up to the living-room of the house on the lake. We brought the easel so it would look more serious, and I shut Gandhi in the attic above my bedroom to avoid any damage. He can sleep on Simon's bed. Simon left behind a smell wherever he went. Ali sniffed around and then he went back to the broom closet with Nagrobis.

We can't sleep. Anne gets into my bed; she snuggles into the hollow of my shoulder. Now we read the Book together, that is, she re-reads to me certain passages that I know by heart. She says each word, slowly, to learn how to make sentences, each with a subject, a verb and an object; it's something she doesn't know how to do except in her head.

My father is here for the last days of summer. He sleeps with my mother and It'saboy in our landlady's bedroom, in the bed that creaks. When my father's not here, my mother puts It'saboy in the bed beside her. When my father is here, she puts my father beside her and It'saboy in a cradle, within reach of her breast. The bed doesn't creak at all when my father sleeps in it, because they both pretend they're asleep while they wait for morning. It'saboy pretends to be asleep, too, but he makes up for it the next day when he has his nap. Actually, he's quiet when the five of us are together. Tonight it's not that Anne and I are pretending to be asleep, it's just that with all the excitement of discovering the painting the next morning, sleep does not come.

~

My mother cries out. My father cries out. In the attic Gandhi barks. It'saboy pounds a wooden spoon against a saucepan. That's what wakes us up because at dawn we finally managed to get to sleep. The Book fell to the floor. I don't like that. The Book is always placed on the chair next to my bed or on a shelf beside the painted piano in my room in town. If the Book is on the ground, that's a bad omen. We don't have to get dressed because last night we didn't undress. We only need to put on shoes and a sweater, because we're cold from lack of sleep. Anne goes down first. I follow her, worried. They are in the living room where It'saboy is making his infernal racket, pounding away to his heart's content. I run back upstairs and let Gandhi out. He is scratching at the door to the attic, something that always infuriates my mother. Gandhi runs at top speed. He manages to make me fall.

I am worried, worried for Anne whom I don't hear laughing or singing or dancing for joy before her reproduction. They are all there, silently looking at the painting on the easel. My father turns to me and says, Plagiary. He takes down the painting and smashes it over his knee. He gets paint on his pants, and he swears very loud. I say nothing. I don't say that Anne spent a month under the verandah making the plagiary. Plagiary, declares my father, is not a "violon d'Ingres"*. The Countess d'Haussonville can go back to her grave. They know nothing about what is under the verandah. They know nothing about the cave of Ali Baba and the forty thieves. They know nothing about life. They don't deserve to know. They don't deserve to understand that they don't understand a thing and that Anne's tears will never dry.

* Ingres, who painted a portrait of the Countess d'Haussonville, was almost as gifted a violinist as a painter; hence "violon d'Ingres" for a secondary pastime or hobby. Trans.

I threw out the Chinese drawing of the line of soldiers. I don't want to know who those letters were addressed to. I return everything to the cellar, to the trunk: envelopes, newspapers, everything except one photo. The photo of the Commander's husband. It's the same as the one in my parents' album, except that at his side, instead of the Commander, stands a very beautiful woman with slanted eyes. That photo will go under my bed with the mask, the ring and Marie Tamponnet's earrings. One day the dust will cover it completely.

~

There is a boy named Élie in my class. I thought it was Ali because of Ali, but I was mistaken. Since I always used to call him Ali, he didn't speak to me at first. Élie looks something like Rajiv but more handsome, taller too, of course, because I haven't seen Rajiv for years. He comes first in class, and he rolls his r's. When he says, It's terrrrible, you feel that it really is terrible. His hands are long and slender, he could play on the red and black keys of my piano; and his nails are carefully manicured and very short. The only thing I don't like about him are his shoes. They aren't walking shoes; they're parade shoes. Because of his shoes he never plays in the schoolyard. I never play in the schoolyard either but not on account of shoes. I don't play on account of my height and my timetable. Other children of my age and height are in grade one, and we don't have recess at the same time.

He stands in one corner and watches with his big dark eyes. The other corners are occupied by two supervisors and me. With my pale eyes I observe his dark ones observing the pupils playing ball or hopscotch. One day I catch him reading the Book. Not mine, his own. For him the Book is homework. He told me so when I took my own Book from my schoolbag. I told him that, for me, the Book is a pleasure and a protection against the men from whom God protects Himself. We become friends. He's my first friend since the time of Esther, a friend I think about at night before I fall sleep and who helps me put up with It'saboy. I only have to imagine we're together, and I forget about my anger or my bad mood.

He is the second son in his family, and his name was the name of his maternal grandfather. He told me a lot about his mother. I haven't told him about mine. He has black curly hair that always smells of jasmine. One day he will let me run my mutilated hand through his curly hair. I think I love him the way I ought to love It'saboy and even more. I love him so much that I don't tell Anne about him. He calls me Fanny, and he tells me he likes the way I look.

He says nothing about his father. I don't ask any questions. He is much older than I, and I don't know if I'll be able to invite him to my room one day. When I ask if he would come, he says yes. If he would come to my bed in the lamplight, with his mouth open all night, he says yes. He understands that I want to drive away dark thoughts. In his house, too, the walls smell of french fries. The smell doesn't have to cross the street, it comes through the ceiling of the restaurant downstairs, through his bedroom floor. He says he wishes they'd fry food that smells like orange blossoms, but orange blossoms don't grow here. We think the same way about the same things.

Pascale told on us, of course. That we hold hands, my left hand in his right, that he's at the head of the class, that he doesn't run because of his shoes. She told about his curly hair that smells of jasmine. Everybody said she was full of hot air. It's her own fault if nobody believes her.

I invited Élie to the house one day when my mother was in the country, visiting her sister with Anne and It'saboy. My mother wanted me to stay behind so I could keep an eye on my father's friends who smoke their cigarettes in rooms where they aren't allowed. I was my father's guardian, and in that role, I could invite whomever I wanted to the house. Élie didn't come on Saturday because in my house we light fires and turn on lights on Saturday. He came on Sunday wearing the right kind of shoes, ones that would be perfectly fine in the schoolyard, if he took the trouble to wear them.

I introduced him to the walls, Gandhi, Ali and Nagrobis, the piano, Nicole, my father, Glenn Gould, the restaurant across the street, my lamp, the photo of my grandfather and the woman with slanting eyes that I took out from under my bed for the occasion and my bed. After that we went to see Malou. There were still some leaves on the trees, which was unusual, leaves of every colour, especially red, that were refusing to fall. We walked for a long time along the paths lined with stones that the names of the people underneath are written on.

Élie said nothing, and neither did I. I was afraid of finding a dead dog. I was afraid Élie would abandon me there for ten minutes, as the Major did, and that I wouldn't be able to find my way back, even though it's a place I know very well. But Élie didn't abandon me. He held my hand tightly in his; he even stroked my mutilated hand, and it tickled.

In front of Malou's hole he got down on his knees and planted a painted stone that he'd brought in his pocket. A stone from his native country for Malou. Instead of the violet now there will be Élie's stone. Stones grow better than violets. The wind blew and some colours fell from the trees. We rolled around in the leaves. People say that they're dead, but that's not true. They don't smell like death; they smell like life, like Aunt Emma's vegetable garden and the urge to laugh.

~

I wanted to take some dried hydrangea blossoms to put in my room, but Élie told me you mustn't pick the flowers of the dead. It's true, if my violet had grown I wouldn't have wanted anyone to pick it, not even after it dried. There are red leaves and blades of grass in Élie's curls. Like a crown. I call him my king; he calls me his queen. We laugh, and I notice that his teeth are very white because his gums are darker than mine. I wonder if everything inside his body is darker than in mine. I also wonder what his tube is like, if it is as alive as It'saboy's.

We didn't bring the Book because Élie had spent Friday night and all day Saturday reading it. He'd had enough of the Book. One day, perhaps, we'll talk about God's son. Like me, Élie is excused from religion class, but he doesn't go to the principal's office. He has permission to spend one hour a day in the library reading his Book.

I had dreamed about him. We were both in the principal's office with the missionary brother I've never met. We were eating a huge gâteau Saint-Honoré while our classmates sang Christmas carols in the schoolyard. I said I wanted to sing with my own classmates, and I went outside through the window. I took flight, like a bird, and Élie tried to capture me with a butterfly net that the principal's brother pulled out from under his soutane. I flew over the heads of my classmates. When they saw me, they all stopped singing, and I fell in the snow. I woke up with a pain in my mutilated hand and the fear that Élie did not really exist.

When we came back from seeing Malou, my father wasn't there. He had made some sandwiches, and we ate them on my bed. I fed the crumbs to Ali and Nagrobis. Gandhi came and lay at the foot of my bed. He always had one eye on Élie. Now the left eye, now the right, as if to say, I've got my eye on you. I wanted to mingle our blood, but Élie didn't want me to mutilate myself with a knife again. We'll wait till it stops oozing. He licked the oozing sore, and then he licked the tears that flowed because I was crying from happiness. It's like laughing till you cry. Just as good. Élie's tongue is soft against my skin.

I didn't tell him I was seven years old. He didn't tell me he was ten, but I knew. One day I asked the principal, who also told me that his father was in jail. His father didn't steal or kill. He is in prison because sometimes life is like that. The prison's not in our town or in our country, so I don't know what his father's prison is like. The principal said it's terrible, but she doesn't roll her r's as Élie does so it doesn't sound all that terrible. If Élie's father didn't kill anyone and didn't rob anyone, he'll get out of prison one day to see his son who will be grown. To see his son period, because he has never seen him. Élie's father has lived in a prison since before Élie was born. It's like that in some families. Prison is like war. It mows down fathers before their children are born.

We slept for a long time in each other's arms. I saw his heart beat in his neck, I saw his eyelids shudder in his dreams, I saw his legs hold my legs tight, I saw his love in every move his sleep allowed him to make. He slept, but I didn't sleep. I was busy loving him.

I put everything away before my mother came home. I didn't want her to notice the jasmine smell of Élie's curly hair. I washed the sandwich plates; I picked up the crumbs Ali and Nagrobis hadn't eaten. I turned off the phonograph, put Glenn Gould's record back in its sleeve, cleaned the dirt off the soles of my shoes and finished the homework I was supposed to do on Saturday. I took care of everything that could have aroused her suspicions.

~

The other day, Anne woke up saying, It's time for it to stop. The sentence wasn't from the Book; it was her own, the first one since she decided to speak only in words that need to be interpreted. It's time for it to stop; where are my socks? She has a low-pitched voice that makes you shiver. Her socks were under her bed. The two of us took It'saboy for a ride in his carriage.

For three days now he has been howling for both of my mother's breasts. As if one weren't enough. It'saboy gets bored; he wants everything of my mother's, her breasts, her husband, her love for us. Anne, who is usually very lenient towards him, is fed up. I push the carriage while she dances around it, singing. Be quiet, It'saboy, be quiet. Listen to me, listen to me. I'm talking now; you can talk later. Leave Mama alone; you're draining her.

She's already deflated, and we still need her. Come and dance with me, It'saboy!

We ran like that all the way to Élie's house. I knew where he lived because I've often followed him home after school. We rang the bell. I was holding It'saboy in my arms; Anne stood there very erect in fifth position. I had to tell her everything about Élie. Another boy who looked like Élie answered the door. He was taller, more like a man. He called Élie, who blushed when he saw me with my children.

It'saboy didn't move a muscle. Élie was very impressed. So was I. I could see that Anne had a cramp. He showed us in. I didn't think the smell of french fries was all that strong. Just a little. It smelled of the steak they grill all day long in the restaurant downstairs. Élie's mother came home with the groceries. She was surprised to see us, and I recognized Élie's eyes and the scent of jasmine when she kissed me. He had talked to her about me.

We don't go to his room, which is at the rear near the back stairs. We stay in the living-room, which is also Élie's mother's room, eating honeycake and drinking milk. It'saboy only drinks my mother's milk, and I have to apologize for him to Élie's mother. She understands and goes to get a rattle. It'saboy smiles. This is the first time I've seen him smile when he's hungry. We'll have to find him a rattle.

We don't say much. Élie shows me around the apartment, except for the bedroom that he shares with his brother. It's very small. There's not much to see: the bed-room, the kitchen, the living-room where we eat honey-cake and the bathroom. I tell him I like his house and his family.

On the way home Anne sings, Fanny's in love! Fanny's in love! I met Fanny's sweetheart. I tell her to be quiet, and she swears that she won't say anything to any-one and says that she's in love with Élie's brother. His name is Ioël. Fanny's in love with Élie, and I'm in love with Ioël! Where are my socks? It'saboy, It'saboy, what a nice name! She's crazy.

~

The Major is losing his marbles. My grandmother is finally going to get the better of her third husband. Since she is older now than she was with her first husband, her chances of finding a fourth are very slim. She won't have a chauffeur any more to drive her to Florida where she can make her pies. That's the only thing she can do well, make pies, and the only thing the Major could do well was to be my grandmother's chauffeur.

He has to be put away in a house for old people who are losing their marbles. I go to visit him with my father every Tuesday evening. If we didn't, the Major would see no one. It wouldn't make much dif-ference because he doesn't recognize anyone anyway. My grandmother went there on the day he moved in, and she doesn't intend to go back until the day he dies.

After our visit to the Major we go to my grandmother's for dinner. She and my father down a number of whiskies. They make up for the years when she acted as if he didn't exist. Sometimes they talk about Francine and a teardrop falls into the little drop of whiskey that my grandmother asks my father to pour. I sit there bored. I leaf through a magazine like at the doctor's and I wait.

Her house isn't as big as the Commander's, but almost. Élie and his family would be very comfortable here. He wouldn't have to do his homework at the kitchen table. He could use the Major's desk, but perhaps then he wouldn't be at the top of his class.

I don't know what will become of my grandmother. She talks non-stop about a rug merchant who is courting her, and I know she's talking through her hat. If it's true then he's a flying-carpet salesman, and I'm the Queen of Sheba.

She's never given me any earrings. She forgot. I rummage in her drawers while they finish their coffee. She has a glove drawer with at least two hundred pairs of gloves in every colour to go with her two hundred dresses of every colour. She no longer wears either her dresses or her gloves because of all the weight she's gained in recent years from eating pies. Whenever she buys a new dress she takes a smaller size in case she loses some weight. My father says it's the weight of the years that has caused it. It's the same for the gloves. I could wear them, but she'll never give them to me. She never gives anything away. My father had to reimburse her for his three months of sickness.

In her bedroom, there's a photo of the two dogs she had before she married the Major. My name for that kind of dog is dog turd. They're long since dead and buried, but she still talks about them as if they were about to jump up on her lap. There are no photos of Francine or the Major or my father. To say nothing of the rest of us.

Every Tuesday I ask myself what I can steal from her to make her mad. I get a new idea every time, and in the dust that's accumulating under my bed are a thimble, a crystal glass, a cake of rose-scented soap, a beach shoe, a fish knife and a rosary. All stolen from my grandmother. I found a box to put them in, along with the other things that have been lying under my bed for years.

She has taught me to play solitaire. I never win, but she always does. I'm sure she cheats, as all grandmothers do. Anne learned from watching me, so we play two-handed solitaire in my bedroom while It'saboy plays with his red truck. But I soon get tired of solitaire, and so does Anne. I would still rather watch her dance.

There are days when I wish I had no family, except Malou who would be my link to the earth. I almost said my native earth because I forget that my native earth is somewhere else. All the same, Malou would be my only link with something that's not altogether native. In a life without a family, Malou would be my friend. A dead friend. Without a family, Pascale wouldn't have cut my hand, my mother would sleep with another father, and It'saboy would have brothers. Without a family, perhaps I wouldn't exist, and that would be fine, except that I wouldn't have the joy of loving Élie. He would certainly meet another girl whose head was plucked and singed, and he'd go on being at the top of his class as if nothing had happened.

~

Uncle Aimard came on business. He comes here on business every year to sell his mink, just the pelts, but this time it's marriage business. He quickly forgot Aunt Emma, and he just got married in our city, because his new wife comes from here. I don't know her, otherwise I would tell her I don't want her taking Aunt Emma's place in Uncle Aimard's bed.

My mother invited him for dinner, and once again the noisy children eat in the kitchen, except that there's no Mathilda or Aunt Emma's raspberry syrup. He lives like a hermit and never gets in touch with anyone. My mother didn't invite Uncle Aimard's new wife. But he told us that Mathilda had married her cousin, as expected, and that she'd had a little girl whom she called Esther.

He brought some mink pelts for my mother. She could have them made into a muff. As he is about to leave he digs around in his pocket and takes out a tortoiseshell comb that Aunt Emma used to wear all the time. This is for you, he tells me. I don't know what I can do with it, with my short hair, but I take it anyway. I'll store it under my bed with the rest while I wait for my hair to grow. It seems as if I'm always waiting for something.

My father wasn't home so Uncle Aimard had a private dinner with my mother, who had put on one of Francine's dresses and her long gold chain for the occasion. She looked so beautiful Uncle Aimard was stunned and forgot to kiss her. I kept my eye on her, the way she'd asked me to keep an eye on my father. I saw her blush, and she didn't say anything when Uncle Aimard lit a cigarette between the salad and the cheese. She even came to get the ashtray she keeps hidden in a cupboard. Beneath her dress you can hardly tell that she has one breast more swollen than the other.

When she came into the kitchen, It'saboy held out his arms to demand her swollen breast, but she gave him his red truck. The cry he was about to let out stayed in his throat. Uncle Aimard left very late, and I was very tired. Anne was already asleep, and It'saboy was howling.

My father came home shortly before daybreak. My mother was in the living-room waiting for him, smoking Uncle Aimard's butts and drinking the dregs of his whiskey. It'saboy had fallen fast asleep on the sofa just as my father used to do when she didn't want him. She was still wearing Francine's dress and her long gold chain. She also had a big ring on every finger, to provoke him. Now and then I would get up to see what she was cooking up for him. She didn't even see me, she was too busy being angry.

He came home shortly before daybreak, fresh as a daisy, clean-shaven, and he told her she looked very beautiful. Her ring-covered hand shot out, too heavy to reach him, and he grabbed hold of her by the waist. Come on, we're going to sleep. That was all he said by way of explanation. He dragged her to her bed, and he got in beside her. It'saboy stayed on the sofa, and I looked after him until I left for school.

It's high time It'saboy learned to drink something other than milk, especially if my mother starts drinking whiskey, too. When I came home at noon, they were still asleep. I took It'saboy in one arm, my schoolbag in the other, and I went to see Élie's mother. I came back for It'saboy at five o'clock. She had bought him a bottle, and he was sitting surrounded by cushions and eating honeycakes. He looked like a potbellied little doll. Next time I'll take him to school with me, with his bottle, to avoid making trouble for everybody.

In the house, joy reigns supreme. Since the dinner with Uncle Aimard everybody has been sick. Anne has stopped going to her dancing lessons because she vomits all the time. It'saboy has stopped playing with his red truck; he sleeps all the time. My father hasn't smoked for a week, and the newspaper calls twice a day about the article he was supposed to turn in a month ago. My mother has lost her voice, and I take her temperature every morning and night as the doctor told me to do.

I have to take Gandhi out, change the cats' litter, do the shopping, fix the meals, wash the dishes, go to school and not think too much about Élie. His mother came the other night to give me a hand because I couldn't take it any more. She told me she wishes she'd had a daughter like me, and I tell her I wished I had a mother like her and long black hair instead of my plucked and singed head and my eyes that are too pale to see properly. Besides, I need glasses. I can't see the leaves on the trees any more or the branches when there aren't any leaves. I can't see the writing on the blackboard or Élie's smile in class. I can barely distinguish an E from an F on my piano on the wall. If this goes on I'll be blind, deaf and mute. I don't mind not being able to see what's around me, but not to hear Glenn Gould or to tell Élie I love him—never!

I got glasses after everyone stopped being sick. They make me look serious, and I'm beginning to see what people look like again. They don't look as good as they do without glasses, except Élie who looks even better. Pascale has a wart on her nose, Simon squints, and my piano needs to be touched up or it will flake.

After his sickness, which didn't last as long as my mother's, my father went away again. He didn't see my glasses, and I didn't see him through my glasses. Perhaps he was afraid. He went away to another country where people are fighting. The newspaper liked his article that came in late and by way of thanks they've sent him to the front. It will mean another Christmas without him, but we're used to that.

~

My mother is peculiar. It'saboy still sleeps in my bedroom, and when he cries at night, I give him his bottle. She wants to sleep, and she doesn't want him to disturb her sleep. It'saboy and I are getting used to one another. To put him to sleep I tell him stories that help me get to sleep, too. The following day he always wants to know what happens next, but I can't remember anything so I have to start again with something else. I don't know if he understands—he's so little—but he demands my stories the way he used to demand the breast.

During the day a lady who reminds me of Aunt Emma comes to look after It'saboy. My mother leaves the house very early every morning, before I've even finished getting dressed. She drives off in a car, well groomed, well dressed, spotless. She comes home just before dinner, which the lady cooks. She unbuttons her blouse and nurses It'saboy. Her breast is full of a whole day's milk and he drinks and drinks while she reads the paper. She doesn't run her hand through his hair now, she doesn't try to make him love her.

I don't know what she is doing. She doesn't tell me anything. She says nothing to the lady, not even thank you for the meals. When she has finished nursing and reading her paper, she takes a shower, then she comes back in a dressing gown, with a towel wrapped around her head. We eat in silence. Anne nods off. I make faces across the table at her and It'saboy, to make them laugh. They laugh, then they stop laughing because of the way my mother looks at them. I know she's tired; I know she can't take any more; I know that the life she dreamed of is a joke; I know she's annoyed with my father. But that's no reason to stop us from laughing at the table.

This year I'd have liked to invite a lot of people to our house for Christmas. Pascale, Simon, my mother's sisters, Uncle Aimard, the principal, Élie, Élie's brother Ioël, Nicole, the lady who takes care of It'saboy: everybody, to put some life into our life. Instead no one came, and my mother stayed in her dressing-gown all day, smoking cigarette after cigarette while she drank the bottle of whiskey she had bought the day before. I'm quite amazed that she smokes now; she used to nag my father about it so much. I don't feel like lighting her cigarettes. It would be just like her to say they're not as good when I light them.

We got permission for the three of us to go to Nicole's. Good thing we have Nicole! She offered us a slice of Christmas log with chestnuts that she'd brought from her parents. It was very good, but Nicole was expecting friends so we left as soon as the doorbell rang. Outside it was snowing. I felt sad for Anne and It'saboy because we hadn't looked up in the sky to watch for the sleigh that belongs to the chief of Christmas who drops gifts down people's chimneys. That's probably why we got no gifts this year. I thought about Esther, Rajiv and Irina one last time. The four of us used to have a lot of fun. I was happy then, and I had a family of mice in the cellar.

~

It'saboy turned one year old, and my hand stopped oozing. My mother was right, nature does take care of everything. The name of the lady who comes every day is Mademoiselle Julie; she and I get along well even though she's not very talkative. I told her not to move the dust under my bed, and she didn't ask any questions. She never does, and she often sings, *À toi belle hirondelle qui viens ici, as-tu vu dans ces îles mon Alexis?* When I ask who Alexis is, she answers with an old smile. I'll never find out, but I shall always remember her song and her old smile.

On Saturday we found Ali lying stiff in the closet. I put her in a bag, and I went off to bury her in Malou's hole. Ali will be company for her. I would have liked to take Nagrobis and Gandhi, too, but no animals are allowed in the cemetery except for dead dogs and cats in paper bags. Anne was crying too much, and I didn't have enough hands to push It'saboy in his carriage, along with the shovel and the cat bag. Élie couldn't come because of the lights and the fire. It's spring now, but there are still circles of snow on the ground. The earth over Malou's hole is muddy and underneath it's harder, as hard as rock.

I scarcely buried Ali, I'll have to come back to put her down deeper. A guard went by just as I was replacing the clods of earth. He asked what I was doing, and I lied. I told him I was planting seeds to make flowers on Malou's hole. He offered to help me but I refused, giving him a sad look. Luckily he didn't see Ali. He would have thrown her into the common grave and called me terrible names. Now Nagrobis sleeps all alone in the closet. It's funny, in this house everybody sleeps alone.

~

When my hand stopped oozing, Élie and I mingled our blood. He took a needle from his mother's sewing kit and a razor-blade from the bathroom. We pricked our left ring fingers and used the razor-blade to make a cross on the tips of our fingers. That way if we marry someone else we'll remember each other when the wedding ring is being slipped on. His finger bleeds a lot, and I'm afraid I cut too deeply. It's not the cut that is deep but the feelings we have for each other. When our fingers stopped bleeding we took off our clothes and mingled our bodies.

This time I was the one who bled. I bled against his skin, onto our legs, onto the white sheet we'd spread on the living-room floor, at the base of the sofa that is also his mother's bed. But I knew it was normal, and I reassured him because he thought I was dying. Our mingled bodies are but a single body, and our joy is great. Now I smell of jasmine like Élie, like his mother, his family, his country. Perhaps I finally have a native land. I didn't want to wash myself, but Élie insisted we go into the water together. I said, This is a baptism. He said, No, it's a purification, and the water and blood will flow into the river to show travellers the way. I didn't understand, but I bathed with him in the water made pink by our mingled bodies. I took the sheet home with me and put it under my bed.

~

My mother works. I know that now. She answers the phone at the university. I can call her, and she can call us. But we never call each other. Her right breast is deflated now; she refuses to give it to It'saboy, claiming she has neither the milk nor the time. She doesn't talk very much about my father who has not come home. He's at the front, that's what everyone says, where they are fighting a war. His weapon is his old Underwood. He never writes, except to his newspaper. I think he's angry now because my mother drinks whiskey and smokes cigarettes just like he does.

She invited a professor from her university for dinner one night, and as we'd done when Uncle Aimard came, the three of us ate in the kitchen with Mademoiselle Julie. I don't know what he told her—I wasn't interested—but she had a faraway look in her eyes, and her cheeks were flaming. I don't trust my mother's faraway look.

Mademoiselle Julie took us out for ice cream. She drove my mother's car because my mother had told her to take us far away, deliberately, so it would take as long as possible to get back. Gandhi came along because the professor is afraid of dogs. I hope he won't go under my bed and take out the sheet with blood on it to spread in the living-room and mingle his body with my mother's.

I have chocolate ice cream, and I get it all over me to shame my mother in front of the professor. Anne does the same and so does It'saboy. Take that, Professor. Mademoiselle Julie is unhappy, what my mother does is none of her business, but she mutters from behind the wheel of the car. She drives fast, to get us home before it's too late. Too late to be putting children to bed, she mutters.

We make a lot of noise coming into the house, and we're surprised to see them still at the table. My mother looks less ecstatic. She is turning a wooden match in her fingers like a magician. With her that's a sign of impatience. Gandhi lies down at the professor's feet, and we have trouble making him move. The professor leaves, furious. You can see it on his face and in the way he doesn't wish us goodnight. The sheet is still under my bed.

~

Since my father has been gone, we don't see the Major any more, and my grandmother phones my mother at the university to say she's ungrateful. My mother is used to that. It's not just the Major who is losing his marbles, she tells us, your grandmother is, too. We'll go to see her on Sunday. That's fine, I'll be able to take something from her as I used to do on Tuesdays with my father.

My grandmother really has lost her mind. She doesn't remember It'saboy, and she tells us she climbs trees because there are too many cars on the street. For once, we enjoy ourselves. Mademoiselle Julie comes with us to wash my grandmother. My mother can't do it by herself because of the weight of my grandmother's years.

My grandmother doesn't talk about the Major or Francine. She talks about her rug merchant and about her mother, who is in the garden, she says. When she is completely naked, her huge breasts float on the water like balloons. I want to touch her, but Mademoiselle Julie holds my hand back. When the Major went to the old people's house, she stopped washing herself so she is very dirty. The water is covered with a grey film that leaves a ring on the tub and on her skin. She has to be rinsed after she's been washed.

She can't wear any of her dresses. My mother makes one for her out of two. She spends a whole day on it. That's all my mother has to do, to make dresses for my grandmother who calls her ungrateful. Before we go I take the Major's pipe. If I see him some day, I'll give it to him.

My mother calls one of my grandmother's cousins to tell her this has to stop. If she goes on losing her mind, my grandmother will die or hurt herself. She's fat from eating nothing but pie and drinking whiskey. The cousin says, All right, I'll do something. But three weeks later, when she hasn't done anything, my mother takes care of it all: finding a house for old ladies with people who will make her eat something besides pie and drink something besides whiskey, and who will wash her once a week.

My grandmother is furious. She shrieks when they come to get her. She hopes my mother burns in Gehenna and gives birth to two-headed children. My mother remains stony-faced, but I know she's cursing my father for not being there.

I return the Major's pipe that day, because now they are in the same house by a river, waiting to die. They're like two strangers. She doesn't remember the Major. She even flirts with him a little at the table when the old people are left by themselves to eat.

After we'd settled my grandmother, my mother and I left there happy. We phoned the cousin to ask her to come and visit because we won't any more, at least not until my father comes home, and that could take time.

~

My father wrote to me:

> He was a handsome young choralist
> Whose name was Pierre or perhaps Baptiste
> The story really doesn't say
> Re Do Ti La So Fa Mi Re
>
> He left his home, went down to the docks
> With one fresh collar and four clean socks
> That's all the baggage he took to sea
> Ti La So Fa Mi Re Do Ti
>
> Away he sailed for England's shores
> But adverse winds blew him off his course
> And he landed in the Congo
> Do Ti La So Fa Mi Re Do
>
> The Queen of this country was dark and tall
> She wore a parasol, that was all
> When she spied our hero she cried "Aha!"
> Fa Mi Re Do Ti La So Fa
>
> "Little-White-Man come over here
> I want to gobble you up, my dear

156

With a bit of garlic and parsley"
Mi Re Do Ti La So Fa Mi

He said, "Wait Madame! You've got me wrong!"
And struck up one of his sweetest songs
The Queen, enchanted, said "Marry me!"
Ti La So Fa Mi Re Do Ti

The moral of this story now:
Let there be music wherever you go
And you may become King of the Congo
Do Ti La So Fa Mi Re Do.

Papa

The letter came from Italy. Nothing to do with the Congo. No return address. There's no war in Italy. I would have liked to write and tell him I wear glasses and that I love Élie. Tell him about Ali's burial, about his mother and the Major being in the old people's house and about how much we miss him. I don't know what his Queen of the Congo looks like, if she's as beautiful as my mother or if she has a piano on her wall where he can make music.

I showed my mother the letter. For once, I couldn't keep a secret under my bed. She turned the envelope over and over, then gave it back to me. I'll stop by the newspaper, she said, they'll know where he is. And besides, I need money.

Mademoiselle Julie has gone home because we can't pay her any more. She would have stayed, but we have our pride, and my mother wouldn't hear of it. We manage as best we can. It'saboy is well behaved, all things considered, and I come home at noon to fix his lunch. Gandhi takes care of the rest. We made It'saboy a house with the armchairs and the sofa. He has his red truck, a rattle and some blocks that used to belong to Élie. Nicole stops by to look in on him when she isn't busy with her friends.

The principal lets me skip study period. I take It'saboy for a walk. There are just a few weeks of school left anyway. Since Élie always comes first, I'm still second, except in history, which is my best subject, and in religion from which I'm excused.

I wrote to the principal's missionary brother who's in Africa not far from the Congo, and I asked him to look for my father. There can't be very many queens in that country; in any case, everyone must know her because queens expect to be known.

My father doesn't need to be told that I wear glasses or that I mingled my blood with Élie's. He doesn't need anything, but I need him. I'll write to tell him that I'm looking for the bastard who has my skin on his skin, who has a face because he took my name on the day I was born. I'll write that I am looking for my wound through all the wounds I've inflicted on myself: the hole in my ear, the cut hand, my belly that bled onto Élie's leg. I'll write and tell him that I could have been the queen of the Congo if only he had wanted it and that I'm a white Negro king because it was what he wanted. I'll write and tell him there is still time for him to carry me in his arms, he who couldn't carry me in his womb, still time before my belly swells up like the dead dog's in the cemetery.

For two days now, Gandhi and Nagrobis have been a sorry sight. My bedroom walls have been painted; the keys of my piano are all white, and so is my piano. I don't play it any more; I've never played it. The red and black piano never existed. Anne brought It'saboy to console me. She tried I tickle your chin and you tickle my chin and the last one to laugh is the winner, but she was the one who laughed all the time. Forced laughter, laughter that doesn't dance, that doesn't roll its r's.

It'saboy gave me a present. One of his blocks: the green one, his favourite, the one that looks like a house because it's the biggest. I don't even say thank you; I just fling it under my bed.

It was my mother's idea to bleach everything white. She's not going to bleach the sheet that has the blood from my body mingled with Élie's. Let her bleach her own; let her bleach her hair or my father's photos if she wants, but not my sheet. I broke Glenn Gould into a thousand pieces to see if the pieces would make music as they fell. The thousand pieces are as silent as my bleached keyboard. How can Anne dance now that there's no music on my wall? I wrote my first letter to Élie. Dear

Élie, I need a painted stone from your native country to plant in my bed. Perhaps music will grow from it to lull my sleepless nights. Fanny.

~

At the end of the school year, there is a performance for the parents. Brothers and sisters who don't go to school are invited, too. Élie and I are going to play a scene the teacher had us rehearse and rehearse for hours and weeks. We know it by heart. Every night before I go to bed I repeat my lines and Élie's, in case he has a blank. Élie does the same. And the next day we rehearse them together on our way to school, and we reverse the roles, with Élie as Antigone and me as the Chorus, just to be sure. I wanted Anne to dance during the scene but my drama teacher said no.

I'm all on edge anticipating our year-end performance. The waiting is the hard part. The closer we come to our big night, the harder it is for my legs to support me on the way to school. Élie has to give me his arm. He encourages me; he tells me I'm the best, that everything will be fine, that I know our lines better than he does, which doesn't reassure me at all.

I've put on one of Francine's dresses. On me it's a long dress. My mother bought me sandals that will be my summer sandals, too. To play the Chorus, Élie is draped in an enormous shawl. He has a wreath of ivy on his head, and he looks like my king more than ever. We tried on our costumes in the principal's office. She adjusted the dress by tying a rope around my waist. It looks prettier that way. I'd like to ask my mother to lend me Francine's long gold chain, but the principal tells me chains like that didn't exist in Antigone's day. Perhaps she wore big rings? Francine's fall off my fingers; I might lose them.

On the night of the performance, I refuse to eat, and my mother has to drive me to the school with Élie because my legs won't support me at all. I have no voice. There are so many students, brothers, sisters and parents in the hall. They all seem to be just waiting for me to lose my voice, to be as mute as my black and red piano that is now white. Élie kisses my forehead and rubs his jasmine curls against my face. There is applause. I'm sitting down; I want to stay sitting down. I am voiceless, I want to remain voiceless. The principal speaks to me; I don't understand what she says.

Be witnesses for me, denied all pity, Unjustly judged! And think a word of love, For her whose path turns, Under dark earth, where there are no more tears. Élie replies, *You have passed beyond human daring and come at last, Into a place of stone where Justice sits. I cannot tell; What shape of your father's guilt appears in this.*

No, this has nothing to do with guilt, with any guilt, I don't want to walk anywhere, I don't want a stage or applause.

We're on now. I stand up. This body is too heavy; it

doesn't stop fleeing from inside. Before the darkness and the silence, I wait. I know they are waiting, too. I'm falling, and I want to break the darkness, to silence the silence, to take flight inside this fall that does not end. *Look upon me, friends, and pity me, Turning back at the night's edge to say, Good-bye to the sun that shines for me no longer.* I advance, and Élie has to hold me back. I advance, and I take flight. Now I understand Malou in her glass house, Malou in her house of earth, Malou who falls into the hole and who took flight. I know the price of the blood that was shed onto the white sheet. *If her death is yours, A mortal woman's, is this not for you, Glory in our world and in the world beyond?* The darkness is scattered; the sandals hurt my feet. I must run now; I must encircle Élie, refuse his arm, look into the void. *Lead me to my vigil, where I must have, Neither love nor lamentation; no song, but silence.* And fall, at last, behind the curtain.

~

Because of my mother's work, we don't go to the house on the lake this summer. We stay in the house on the street, without a piano, without a father. With the money the newspaper gave us, Mademoiselle Julie came back. I buy the newspaper every day to read the letters from my father. He seldom writes so I often read it for nothing, even the stories about stray dogs and dead people, just in case.

He goes to every country in the world except to mine and the Congo. One day he is in Élie's country, and I wish that he had talked about Élie's father and about the other fathers who have been in jail since before their sons were born. But all the stories are about bread and kings.

One day he wrote, My daughter, and I wondered if he remembered me. Another day he wrote, My son, and I knew he was remembering It'saboy.

Every day I go swimming in the pool with Élie. Anne comes too if Ioël does. She tripped on a beachball and cut her head open on the blue cement. I saw blood in the water that reminded me of the blood in the bathtub for guiding travellers. She swallowed a lot of water and blood, and it had to be taken out before she was rushed to the hospital.

Now she can't swim any more because there is a plaster cast on her head, and it's much too heavy. She can't swim, and she has to be fed with a spoon. We have to make faces so she will open her mouth. If she doesn't open her mouth to eat she opens it even less to talk. I know already that she's going to go start talking in riddles again!

My grandmother is an idiot. She got angry at everybody, and she hit the Major with her cane. Poor Major! She's had a cane ever since her craziness in the tree. With all her weight, all her stubbornness, she hoisted herself up to the second branch of the apple tree in the garden of the old people's house. She wanted to play captain and cross the ocean at the prow of her ship. If I'd been there,

I would have told her that captains, the ones I know anyway, are a little more dignified than that.

She fell from her lookout post and broke her leg. Apparently all the old people applauded because she gets on their nerves. When she started walking with her cane, they made themselves very small. She frightens everybody but the Major, who has lost his marbles. And wham! with her cane on the Major's head. It bled. Now she has to be locked up. I know I'll never get the earrings she promised me.

Her cousin came for the house, and everything inside it. She will put the things in her own house, which is even bigger than my grandmother's. I wanted the photo of my grandmother's dogs, but it had disappeared. I wanted a pair of gloves, but she'd taken them all, even though they don't fit her, and they never will.

Since my father went away, we've had nothing to say about my grandmother's affairs, and my mother doesn't want to look after them. She wants nothing to do with my father's family. I sometimes wonder if she wants anything to do with her own family. I don't mean her sister or Pascale and Simon; I mean us, her children, I mean Anne's head that is getting smaller under her plaster hat, I mean the fact that It'saboy isn't talking, that he hasn't learned how to say even the tiniest little word since he came into the world, despite my attempts to interest him in words, despite the hours I spend telling him stories and putting up with his begging for what comes next by stretching out his arms the way he used to do for my mother's breast. She doesn't even realize that my eyesight is deteriorating. It seems as if she's only interested in the calls she gets at the university and the time that passes when she doesn't work on Saturday and Sunday.

Besides making everything in the house white, she is throwing out everything that belonged to my father. I tell her not to; I tell her he'll come back, that he wrote to us in the newspaper. But she doesn't listen to me. She stuffs everything into big canvas bags and dumps them outside. From my window, I have seen men and women slit the bags; take out books, neckties, shoes, pants, in broad day-light; try them on, too. The women were taking the books; the men were taking men's things. And what about when he comes back? We'll start again. In the meantime, it smells of mildew, and I don't want anything that smells of mildew in my house. This is my house, too, I tell her, and my father's. She can't take it away from me. Even he cannot take himself away from me.

I went out on the street to pick up the only thing the men and women had left: an old inkwell with its cover missing.

~

The children and the animals were having a nap because of the heat. Mademoiselle Julie answered the door. There's a lady, she told me, a lady with a peculiar accent; I can't understand what she wants. Please come and talk to her. Oh yes, I forgot, she has eyes like almonds. No, no, Mademoiselle Julie, you don't say eyes like almonds, you say almond eyes, like Malou's, like the Chinese, like babies still in bellies before they're born.

My heart was beating very fast. Almond eyes and a funny accent: What if it's Malou? Malou who hasn't learned to talk yet, Malou who can't make herself understood, Malou in the skin of a lady, Malou a lady because you grow faster in the ground? Could Élie's stone have brought Malou back to the land that is hers? Is it possible that Élie's stone is more powerful than the glass house and the doctors who helped Malou cling to life?

I left my Book, I ran to the door, I wanted to see, I wanted to hear, to hope, to believe.

The lady was waiting, sitting in a chair. Her back was to me. I saw first her big hat, a hat like the ones I found in the forbidden cellar of the house on the lake. And white gloves that the lady had draped on her lap. Madame! She turned around.

I know her, she hasn't changed. She isn't smiling quite so much, that's all; she's younger, too. I am sitting across from her, and I don't say anything till Mademoiselle Julie finally leaves the room. Then we talk. First the lady, slowly so I can understand, with great economy of gestures so as not to frighten me. She wants to see my father; she wants to tell him about a death. When she says death, tears glisten in her almond eyes. She says that we have the same name, she and I, that her grandfather was also my father's grandfather. She says that I could have been her daughter. She is my aunt. Now I understand about Malou's eyes, it's not all that complicated, it runs in the family, the Chinese family of the Commander's husband. Her name is Kuo-Yuen for those who are entitled to know. And you, you are Fanny with your eyes that contain tragedy. The house beside the lake is her house. The cellar there is the story of my great-grandfather.

My father has gone away. He has gone away, and he keeps coming back and back, in my nights, my days, even though my mother fills canvas bags with his socks and his detachable collars. He'll come back, I'm sure of it, and so will Kuo-Yuen when he comes back. I know Kuo-Yuen's father; he's the man from Chinatown. I won't see him again; he died just as my father had said. He is dead, and his daughter is sad. I'm sad, too, because it's as if my own father were dead. He never talked to me about you before. Or after. So I don't know very much. I know that Malou had almond eyes and that she is in a hole and that there are dresses and jewels in the cellar of the house beside the lake, and mice.

When Kuo-Yuen left she took the inkwell that was missing its cover.

167

When he wrote, My wife, I knew he was going to come home. He would have written, My queen, if he'd been talking about the Queen of the Congo. My wife meant my mother and all the children.

The newspaper called. He's coming. Prepare yourselves; he has changed a great deal. We have, too, but not as much as he has. He looks as old as the Major, except he still has all his marbles.

He arrived one Saturday morning on a bed with wheels and with tubes in his arms like Noah. If my mother hadn't told me, Kiss your father, I would have kissed a stranger. He calls me Fanny. It's the first time he has ever called me Fanny. When he saw It'saboy he murmured, He's a fine-looking boy, and when he saw Anne, he told her, You don't look very well.

My mother has made up the bedroom with white sheets that have the good smell of sheets dried outside on a clothesline. She hasn't put on blankets because of the wounds. They lay him on the big bed, the one where she used to sleep without him. She is waiting. You don't look all that well yourself, she tells him, and he laughs.

He is missing some teeth. That's not serious; you can always get others. I wonder what he'll wear when he is able to pull on a pair of trousers, because people in our neighbourhood are wearing his pants now. Perhaps I can ask them to give them back to us.

He came home without anything. I mean totally naked, wearing just his bandages, the ones they put on him over there. I don't know where 'there' is; I don't know who 'they' are. But he's home. He smiles when he talks, For the time being, he says. He has bouts of malaria that aren't serious, but they wet his sheets. We have to change them, and I know it hurts because he grimaces. There is nothing we can do but wait. He refused to wait in the hospital, saying that he will smash everything. I wonder how he would do that.

The bandages are for his wounds. Where? In the war. Yes, but where are his wounds? Ah! His legs, his tube, his stomach. Apparently his whole stomach came out. They put it back inside, a little crooked my mother says, laying her hand gently on his chest. As for the legs, they don't know if he'll be able to walk with them again. As for the tube, it's as if he doesn't have one.

It will take him six months. It will take us a whole lifetime.

The newspaper sends flowers. There's a constant coming and going in the house, because of the nurses who watch over him day and night. We can't do anything; we can't even jump on his bed.

The nurses whisper. I don't like that. I stick out my tongue at them, and It'saboy sets the dog on their heels when they've finished their watch and are going home, after washing their hands just like that. They whisper, they change bandages. I am never there when they do it.

They ask Mademoiselle Julie for water; they take my
mother aside and tell her it would be better to send him
to the hospital before sending him to his death. Never.
She's strong, my mother. Her man has come home; he
won't go away again even if she did throw out all his
things in her anger with him. They already have long
faces, as if they were undertakers in their spare time.

Apparently the house is a better place to die in,
except that he's not going to die. I know that, it's what I
want. To prove it, I make Anne dance with her plaster
hat, and I make her talk. Now she can feed herself, and
soon she'll be healed. Just like him. If she can be healed,
he can at least make an effort to live.

My mother no longer answers the phone at the university. She is on leave until further notice. If my col-
leagues call to ask, tell them that. She is there for every
hour of my father's struggle for life. It's not the same
struggle as Malou's when she was trying to cling to life.
Malou never talked; he tells us stories, when he's not too
exhausted from the fever.

He asked me to read a passage from the Book. I
couldn't. I was crying behind my glasses, my lips were
quivering, and my voice was very small. I held out the
Book for my mother, but she closed it because my father's
eyes were shut. She talks to him a lot while he's asleep.
She says nice things like, I love you, which I've never
heard her say before.

My mother's hair is all white. Mademoiselle Julie told

us it was fear of losing him that had made it turn white. His hair is white too. I won't lose him—I'm sure of it—and my hair won't turn white.

He told us about the whistling, the crying, the explosion and the dead all around him. He played dead like the dead, with his stomach outside. They came looking for him at night. I don't know who 'they' are. He remembers the smell and the flies. The burns all over his whole body that is a thousand times hotter than the hottest summer day. Just try to imagine that. He had known the dead when they were alive. They were his friends. They died for the cause. What cause? The cause of the smallest people. I didn't know children had their own martyrs.

One day he stopped telling us stories. My mother stayed beside him, lying there in the bed. She had her hand on his chest, always, as if to prevent life from escaping. But no, life doesn't escape just like that, after so much laughter, so many promises. It's impossible. Life is hiding, that's all, because it is weary. And when it is too weary to hide any more, life will go back under all his bandages; it will flow in his veins. And if he wants, we'll mingle our blood, which is already mingled.

His friends from the newspaper came and brought a bottle of whiskey. They showed me how to play cards, how to win with a bad hand, how to spend hours waiting for time to pass surrounded by smoke and empty bottles. Mademoiselle Julie made them black coffee, and they gave the children a kiss before bidding my father farewell.

Because of the latest events I know now that God is a lie, but I can't prove it, just as I can't prove the existence of God. If God is a lie, life itself is a lie, and so are all people and all things. The entire earth has lived a lie as long as it has existed, and so do those who inhabit it. That is why death exists. It doesn't explain the joy of Anne, who danced tonight. And I don't understand anything any more. I should talk with Élie about it, but I'm afraid that doubt and apprehension would creep over him too. If Élie told me, God is not a lie, you can believe in Him, it would be very awkward. Do we have to believe in a thing that is not a lie? All I know is that it's possible to believe in something that is a lie.

I have a question to ask my father. He must wake up. He must hear me. I have two questions, actually. It has been dark for so long. I slip into his bedroom. Gandhi growls; I signal to him to be quiet. A girl has the right to talk to her father who is going to die. No, he's not going to die. They're both asleep. Life rises and falls in his chest. My mother's hand rises and falls along with it. It is the hand of a woman who is grasping at life while she sleeps.

Speak to me, answer me, can you hear me? Life rises and falls, faster now. Tell me, who was that Queen of the Congo? He opens his eyes and smiles. I knew he could hear me. Who was she, who was the Queen of the Congo? Life summons up all its strength and finds a passage between his lips: It was you. You were my Queen of the Congo.

And tell me again, while life is at your lips, tell me, if I make a girl for you and give you her placenta, the way you gave away mine, and plaster it over your whole body, even on your tube, will you be healed? Life spoke again. In a breath, life said to me, Yes, and then life laughed, very softly.

One night he utters a tremendous cry. If the great horned owl had cried out, he would have cried that way to summon his forest. My father's forest is right there beside him. It hears him; it opens its arms to him.

~

Élie has given me two more painted stones. One for my bed and one for my father. Dear Élie, Too late, I don't have a bed now, I don't have a father any more. Fanny.

~

In my new bed in my new house, I spend all my time under the covers. I make a tent there, using clips and a broom handle, and I stay inside it, sheltered from the light. I stay there with my dark thoughts and the memories of the dead. I bundled up the sheet streaked with blood and put all my artillery inside it: the two painted stones, the green block, the comb, the carnival mask, the earrings, the shoe, the soap and other things of no importance. If I hadn't given Kuo-Yuen the inkwell, I'd have put it there, too. The blood-smeared bundle is at the back of my closet, and when I'm ready, I'll tie it to my broom handle and go away. The principal came to see me. She spoke to me through the opening I'd fixed up, for letting the plates in at suppertime. She told me her brother was coming soon and that he asked about me often in his letters. She told me she had been making a lot of spelling mistakes since I'd stopped reviewing what she wrote and that she was ashamed to be a school principal who makes spelling mistakes. She gave me a note from the religion teacher, but I don't want to read it. I'm sure he wrote, I am praying for you or something like that. As if you could pray for someone other than God. There is also the bouquet of jasmine Élie sent me. A bouquet of jasmine that doesn't smell of jasmine because it's too old, too dry. I don't want to believe that one day Élie will no longer smell of jasmine, like this bouquet, because he'll be too old and too dry. When that day comes, jasmine will stop flowering. I hear my mother tossing restlessly. Every night she tosses restlessly and flings herself onto the floor. Then she gets up and goes to It'saboy's room to give him a kiss. Now that each of us has a bedroom, It'saboy falls asleep with his eyes open, as if he were expecting to see my father suddenly appear. My mother kisses him and shuts his eyes, the way you shut a dead person's eyes, the way they did to my father after the cry to the forest. I can hear her tossing. I count to a thousand. That's how long it takes for silence to return. Then

I think about Christ on the cross and the sorrow his father must have felt when Christ asked him, Why? Why have you forsaken me? The father's sorrow must have been even greater than the suffering of the son. I can hear Anne talking to Malou, and Malou answering her. I wonder how she can come out of her hole like that every night. The road is so long. She's so small! Anne and Malou laugh together; I wish I could be with them. When I finally do decide, it's always too late, and I'm not brave enough to emerge from my tent to waken Anne. I can hear Élie. I know it's daytime; it can't be Saturday because of the light and the fires that are being lit here. He is talking to me, and I don't understand. I'd have liked him to tell me that you can't believe something if it's a lie. His voice has changed. It's deeper now. He must have grown. I nearly asked him to take the bundle and throw it in the river, in the ravine behind my house in the other town. I recognize the passage from the Book that he is reading to me. I want to cry. He has brought me paper and pencils. I know now what I must do. I want blood to flow between my legs, my blood mingled with the blood of Élie, of Esther, of Rajiv and Irina. It's time now for me to hurl my body into a hole.

Coach House Press
50 Prince Arthur Avenue #107
Toronto, Canada   M5R 1B5